Earned by the
BILLIONAIRE

Book 1 of the Earned Series

by Shani Greene-Dowdell

This book is dedicated to anyone who gave love a second chance.

PROLOGUE

RUSTY

"Live," were Paula's final words to me. But how did she expect me to live when a part of me was actively dying? I walked out of the hospital and toward my car. Distraught over Paula's condition, my vision was a blur. I couldn't move on like she wanted me to. I needed her to survive... for me. For us. Our love was supposed to be forever. How could she leave me like this?

I drove away from the hospital in a daze. How I made it home was a mystery. I couldn't remember one single thing about the drive home. My mind was numb as I walked through my front door, headed straight to my office, and pulled out the chest that held the remnants of my life with Paula. Inside was her favorite hair clip. I held it in my hand, then ran my free hand over a pair of golden earrings. I gave the earrings to Paula when I started having serious feelings for her. Her grandmother's wedding ring was inside the chest. Each of these items meant the world to Paula.

When I picked up the last letter she wrote to me, my heart sank.

Rusty, My Love...

4

It is with a bleeding heart and trembling fingers that I write this note. Tears fill my eyes that will not fall because I know lying flat on my back I will never be the woman I want to be for you. I beg and plead that you let me go. For you to not torment me any longer with our past. Allow me to transcend into the next phase of my life to what is and what will be inevitable, eternal sleep until you awaken me in heaven to let me know you've arrived to join me.

As I lay here in a dysfunctional body, I have watched your pain for me. I have watched your tears fall. I have heard your sniffles in the night. I know how hard this is on you, and I can no longer find it in myself to be a burden. At thirty-nine, you're still young. You are handsome. You are loving. You are genuine. You are God-fearing. And, yes, you are mine. Mine to set free.

I appreciate you for the times we shared. Now, I ask you to let me go. Allow me to go to a nursing home or some type of facility where they will take care of me until my time is up.

Most importantly, I do not want you to come here anymore to visit me. I mean it, I do not want you to step foot on the property. It breaks me to know you love me and I can't be there for you. My heart burns with pain to say I don't want you anymore because I do. I want you. It's not that my heart doesn't beat in sync with yours because it does. I just can't live through this pain with you. If it continues, I will surely die because of how this has broken us.

I would feel much better if I didn't have to see that pitiful look in your eyes when you look at me. It devastates me to think about everything I can't give you every day as I lay here an invalid. I never wanted our love story to end this way, but this is what we have and I *would much rather imagine you in a better place. My heart would dance and tickle with joy knowing you can go on with your life and find true love again.*

Rusty, I don't want you to have any reservations in finding someone who will love you from the top of your curly head to the bottom of your silken ivory toes and everything in between, which is wonderful, genuine, and loving. I don't want you ever to think I didn't love you with my whole heart.

Knowing my heart, you know this comes from a real place. I know you will resist this, but just take one look into my eyes after reading this note, and you will see these are my true feelings. I love you enough to free you, so please love me enough to let go.

The day will come when we will dance again. We will laugh together again. We will smile, and we will rejoice in one another when we meet again in heaven. But for now...today... we must let go. You must let me go.

My sincerest plea,

Paula

Tears fell profusely the first day I read the letter. Knowing Paula poured her heart into it hurt like hell. When I looked at her, she seemed so confident in what she'd written. Her eyes were emotionless, all business. Paula had given up on us, just like she gave up on overcoming her health battles. I remember walking over to her bed and dropping down beside it, pulling her hand into mine.

"I can't let go," I told her.

She didn't wrap her fingers around mine. She wiggled them out of my grasp as she shook her head. Her heart rate increased, and the monitor started beeping loudly—the sign that she wanted me to leave.

She'd succumbed mentally to being a paraplegic with respiratory and stomach injuries. I, on the other hand, held onto the last fiber of hope, as I would until the very moment she took her last breath.

I never once believed Paula wouldn't walk out of that hospital. I never even imagined it a possibility. Even as I re-read the letter she gave me a month ago, I still didn't want to believe it. To know the woman I cherished as bone of my bone, flesh of my flesh, would never stand on her own two feet, bear my children, go to dinner or make love to me again... wrecked me. But to be exiled from her life, knowing my mere presence hurt her physically, broke me even more.

I was stuck trying to figure things out on my own. I had no choice but to move forward without Paula, whose body reacted violently simply because I came near her. I didn't know where I would go from here. How to live. How to love again. I didn't know what to do.

CHAPTER ONE

RUSTY

Where is the Love?

One Year Later

"Thanks for spending the evening with me," I said with a half-hearted smile.

An increasingly familiar hollow feeling settled in my chest as I closed the door on my latest one-night stand. I'd had a no-strings-attached arrangement with a mild-mannered brunette I'd met at the bar. Our meeting had been a perfect situation for us both. She equally needed love but not a commitment, and this was something I willingly provided for her. We shared a give-take moment of fulfillment, but now that she was gone, I started to forget what she looked like, her name a mere blur. I think it was Cindy, or maybe it was Cheryl. Who knew?

After a few seconds of contemplating, I figured there was no reason to rack my brain over the unimportant details of our encounter. After all, like so many women I brought home, we'd both agreed it would be nothing more, nothing less than a casual fling. Names didn't matter in the grand scheme of things. This had been the way I preferred it since the only woman I allowed close to me, after Paula tossed me out of her life, had stuck it to me in a major way.

My heart ached for months after Paula exed me from her life. It took some effort to get over her, but I eventually tried to move on when a cute, little, talkative, social butterfly named Meagan caught my attention. Her father worked in my social circle, and I fell for her the first time we met. Blessed with Paula's oval facial structure and long flowing blonde hair, she looked good on my arm at parties and could hold a conversation. She had a way of making you feel like you'd known her for years. That came in handy when I needed someone to talk me to sleep each night—someone to help me forget Paula, if only for a few hours. A peaceful sleep had become a thing of the past before I met Meagan.

The more I got to know Meagan, the more things didn't add up. One minute, I thought we were in love; the next, I felt like she was only after my money. Thankfully, I found out our relationship was a farce before I made the mistake of giving her my last name. Benefits came with the last name von Strauss—one being the entitlement to the fortune I worked tirelessly to build. I didn't want to hand that over to just anyone.

After the pummeling my heart took from being exiled from Paula's life, Meagan's deceit broke me even more. I had been on the brink of changing my life for her. I found the perfect ring and was dead-set on fulfilling the promise I made to Paula, the promise to start my life anew with another woman.

Anger rose in me as I thought of Meagan. Admittedly, I wasn't wildly in love with her, but I was getting there. I trusted her. I opened up to her. I'd felt ready to spend a life together, but she was a wolf in sheep's clothing. Marriage was sacred, only to be embarked upon by two insanely in-love people who fully trust each other.

Tears for Paula built in my eyes, but I dared to let them fall. I missed her. I wanted to talk to her. If only I could smell her one last time, it would carry me over for years to come. Years I never imagined I would have to spend without her. Years, I had to power through life without her.

Without my beautiful wife, I had to settle with being a high-powered, innovative entrepreneur by day and single and ready to mingle playboy by night. It wasn't ideal. It wasn't what I dreamed of when I put the ring on Paula's finger so long ago, but it was my life. And it worked for me.

Except, apparently, now it didn't.

Despite all my efforts to ignore it, the feeling of emptiness plaguing me slowly got worse. Business was better than ever. We made a name for ourselves in social media technology. My social calendar was full. I checked all the boxes for a happy bachelor. So what was making me feel empty? What was I missing?

*

"Love," my executive assistant and dear friend, Cassandra, said as she handed over my coffee the next morning.

I'd made it into the office and was failing miserably at getting a productive day started. Startled by her intrusive voice, I glared at her before I spoke, "Love?" I repeated, panic already starting to tighten my chest as I said the word. Did she know something I hadn't shared? Hardly, but I sat up straighter in my chair to see if she'd be more forthcoming with her insight. "What are you talking about, Cassandra?"

She picked up on my expression and rolled her eyes. "Oh, calm down, Romeo, I didn't mean love as in relationship love. You're *so* not ready for human love. I was thinking more like a pet."

"A pet?" Oh, if that was all she meant, I could relax. I'd dodged a bullet. Still, my brow lowered into a skeptical frown. "What are you saying exactly?"

"I'm talking about what you need, boss. I think you need to find love."

"Need to find love?" I echoed.

"How you got to be Chicago's most innovative tech guy when all you do is parrot people, I'll never know," she teased and then snorted out a giggle. "Yes, a pet. You know, cat, dog, goldfish?"

"All I need is energy, so thanks for the coffee. How is my getting a cat, a dog, or a goldfish supposed to help me anyway?"

"It'll give you something to focus on when you're not busy becoming the world's richest man, building your corner on the internet, or trying to get laid."

I smirked. "Cassandra, you should know by now that I don't have to *try* to do anything. I'm either getting laid or in mogul mode. Both are excellent choices of things to do in a day, in my opinion."

"Uh-huh, if you say so." Cassandra arched a brow and shot me a smirk of her own.

My teeth flashed as my lips split into a wicked grin. "I already said so." My smile faded into contemplation. "I always wanted a dog, but getting one would mean taking care of it. Feeding, watering, walking, and what if it got into my closet? Can you imagine what a dog would do to my designer shoes?" The thought of a furry little animal running around my all-white house tearing up my things was a turn-off.

"So lock your closet and teach it not to chew on your things," she replied with a shrug. "If you're scared that it's too much responsibility, you could always start with a ficus. I hear they're very gentle and easy to tend to."

I glared at Cassandra.

She fluttered her eyelashes, mocking me.

"Whatever, I'll think about it," I said.

"That's a start."

"Maybe I could hire someone to take care of the dog."

"That would defeat the purpose of buying it, Rusty. It's supposed to be your little companion. Someone you can come home to at the end of the day and bond with."

"We'll see," I nodded at her.

She took that as her cue to get back to work.

The thought of a furry little animal with big eyes waiting for me by the door wasn't so bad. The little fellow might love me unconditionally, unlike Meagan.

An hour later, I was looking up ads for dogs. I saw quite a few that didn't interest me. Then, I came across one that caught my attention: a brown cocker spaniel. It had been the eyes that sold the dog. I picked up my cell and sighed before calling the owner to make arrangements to get the dog. We agreed to meet at Vinny's Cafe on Michigan Avenue. It seemed like a farfetched idea, me owning a pet, but Cassandra might be on to something. A dog could offer me affection without the same commitment of having a woman around.

Forty-five minutes later, I left the office to meet the dog's owner at the diner. I got out of the limo and strolled down Michigan Avenue. It felt chilly out, so I pulled my scarf tightly around my neck and stuck my hands into my pockets.

As I walked down the sidewalk toward the café, I contemplated whether I was really about to get the animal. Without realizing I'd stopped, I stood in front of Jazzy's Boutique, recalling two weeks ago when I stood in this very place and admired a strikingly gorgeous woman. I put my hand against the glass and studied the items elegantly adorning a slender mannequin... the same ensemble she had been looking at that day.

I was late for my appointment with the dog owner, but it could wait. Memories of Kayla's curly, dark brown hair down to her booted feet took over my mind. She wore a knee-length fur coat and leggings underneath a cute blue dress. It would've been hard to miss her lovely build. As amazingly statuesque as she was, the only thing moving my attention from her physical attributes was the shiny object lying near her foot. The stray piece of jewelry gave me the perfect opportunity to lean down next to her. The view from behind her was impeccable, but I needed her to turn and face me.

I picked up her earring. *"Ma'am, I think you dropped this."*
"Thank you," she muttered sexily.

My insides lit up. Her sweetness caused something to shift inside of me. I didn't know what made me ask her out for a cup of coffee, but I felt relieved when she nervously accepted my offer. I gave her my business card to call and set up a time, and I hadn't heard anything else from her.

Remembering her delicate features and luxurious fragrance, I knew exactly what I needed, and it wasn't an animal as Cassandra suggested. I retreated to my limo for the ride home, her innocent smile permeating my thoughts. Maybe time with Kayla would prove she was what I needed.

Kayla, why haven't I heard from you?

Wait. Why was I still thinking about her? If she called, she called. If not, I would get over it. She was just a random woman. They all were.

After losing my one true love, my oath to never love again rushed into my mind in an attempt to fight any new feelings from surfacing. New women were supposed to be something to do, a passage of time. I never planned to love another. My meant to be love had come and gone. This much, I was sure of.

I wasn't looking for love again. Giving my heart away yielded consequences that I wasn't willing to pay for the second time. I wined and dined the best of them. I crushed women for breakfast and sent them on their way before lunchtime.

Yet, no matter how much machismo I pumped into myself, the memory of Kayla's essence wrapped itself around me in a vice grip. The thought of sitting across the table from her and sharing a coffee made me smile. I rested my head on the seat, and let out a deep sigh, willing my mind to think about something else.

I made it to my neighborhood before I thought about that dog again. I called and apologized to the dog owner and hung up. Oh well, Cassandra's idea for me to find a pet had taken me to Michigan Ave. However, it had been the memory of an intriguing stranger that put a smile on my face. Admittedly, seeing her smiling face in my home would do more for me than a furry little friend.

CHAPTER TWO

KAYLA

Good Riddance

The "walk of shame" to my boss's office was torture. I prayed she wouldn't say anything to upset me when I told her I needed to leave early. I wouldn't be able to take the high road today. If she tried to be a smart ass, it wouldn't fare well for either of us. She humiliated me before when I had personal matters come up during office hours, but no, not today!

"I have a personal emergency that I need to deal with immediately," I got straight to the point when I entered Helen's office. I didn't have time to hem-and-haw over the reason I needed to leave. "My job is caught up and Sandra is covering my phone line," I added, letting her know I'd handled my business before I approached her.

She peered over the rim of her glasses. Then she made a grating sound with her teeth as if the sight of me had gotten on her last nerve.

I turned to leave.

"Kaaaylaaaa," she drew out my name with a long, exasperated sigh. Sitting in her high-back chair, she wore a pair of bifocals and a messy brunette ponytail piled at the top of her head. "What could be going on with you now?"

Well, she could have pretended to give a damn about my emergency. Instead, she acted as if I habitually took time off from work. I spun back around to face her. "As I said before, it's personal. I prefer not to discuss the details right now."

Her piercing eyes peered at me. "I'm your boss, so I have the right to know what's going on before I approve for you to leave."

I stared at her in disbelief. "The only other time I've requested to leave early was when my mother was sick and I needed to get to Alabama ASAP. Thankfully, that was on a Friday and I was back at work on Monday. I don't know why my needing to leave now is a problem." I didn't have a habit of dodging work. I kept my time off to a minimum so that I wouldn't have to hear her mouth about it.

"But you were just out on..." She flipped the calendar hanging on her wall back a few months. "August second with a summer cold."

"That was two months ago and I had the flu. What do you want me to do when I'm ill? Come in here and spread germs everywhere?" I asked, knowing she would do that if it had been her.

She rolled her eyes and raised one finger to touch her temple. "I suppose it doesn't matter at this point. If you have to go, you have to go."

Bingo! My past illness didn't matter, so why was she bringing it up? I cocked my head to the side and pushed back the thoughts in my mind. Holding on to the last strand of tact inside of me was hard to do. "We are given the sick time to use when we are sick, right?" I asked.

"Yes."

I tried to tamp down my anger as I continued, "And I have enough sick time to cover leaving today, so why did you bring up my sickness from two months ago?"

"You know what, go ahead and go, Kayla," she said, repositioning her glasses on her nose. "But consider yourself warned. The next time you have to leave midday without a valid reason will result in a write-up. We are too busy for you to keep running off on your 'emergencies.' " She used air quotes around the word.

If I had cosmic powers, I would use them to string her up by her unruly ponytail. She'd be hanging from the same nail of her credentials on the wall. Without replying, I turned on my heels and stormed out of her office. I really didn't have the time or energy for Helen's power tripping today.

"Ugh!" My spiked heels clicked against Naustram Media Agency's shiny, marble floors as I rushed toward the exit. With each step I took, I only could think of one thing. *Ju had better have a good reason for not going to work today.*

If he had quit another job, I would lose my mind when I got home. I'd deflected my anger to my boss, but Julius "Ju" Martin, my live-in boyfriend, was the real culprit for my ill mood.

My best friend/roommate called me minutes ago to tell me he was at home playing video games. She thought she was home alone, but he startled her when he waltzed into the kitchen to get a snack and told her he was laid off again. For Ju, that meant he didn't get out of bed on time and was fired, which would be my last straw!

I couldn't believe he didn't go to work. He promised he would do better and made love to me last night to seal the promise. It hurt to know I couldn't trust him to honor his word.

On the drive to my apartment, I ran a mental assessment of my relationship with Ju. He acted as if he didn't have a care in the world, and this unsettled me.

Why did I love him so much? I was too ambitious to settle for his ways that had damn sure set in by now. I put too much hope into him, defended him against my parents' disapproval, and what did Ju do to thank me, except hand me a shitload of excuses?

My parents hadn't looked at me the same since I started dating him. They saw straight through him the first time they met him. My father summed him up in minutes, and every time I went to Alabama to visit, he would lecture me about how I deserved better.

"Baby girl, if a man can't give you this," Dad said as he pointed at our meal spread out on the table, *"then he don't deserve nunna yo' time."*

My mother sat right alongside him, talking about how I didn't make Ju earn me. "Just gave him the whole damn cow for free," she'd said as she looked at me with the deepest disappointment in her eyes.

I'd grown tired of listening to their anti-Ju sermons. I was over their disappointment in me. They made me feel like choosing Ju was a sad reflection of my character. And now, I believed them. How could I combat what they said about him when he continuously proved them right?

I should've waited for my soulmate to find me. I met Ju at a nightclub and invited him home for a night of fun. I fell for his dimpled smile, smooth brown skin, and listening ear. His encouraging kisses and warm embrace cemented my feelings over the following months. Nothing made me fall for him more than his melt in your mouth, handsome face, and kingly stature. His strong jawline, deep-set eyes, thick brows and luscious, kissable lips could make a woman forget her problems. So I overlooked all of his problems...the biggest challenge being his unwillingness to provide for himself.

But he could play that damn video game in the streets from now on. Ju had to get the hell out of my apartment. He had to be delusional to think he could get away with getting fired again. No, I wasn't running a free soup kitchen and lodging. A good work ethic was a requirement for him to be my man. He couldn't seem to get it together because he spent most of his time entertaining himself with the latest movie or video game.

The tires of my 2020 Chrysler 200 screeched as I came to a halting stop in the parking space beside his 1994 Grand Prix. His poor car needed everything to get it going daily—water, oil, brake fluid, a jump. But the man was too caught up in video game land to make the eight dollars an hour he needed to buy a battery.

He'd rather wait for me to get home, so he could use my car and debit card for the things he needed. I had to admit I'd spoiled a grown man for a whole year. I helped in the creation of a man-child.

Well, no more.

The more I thought about it, the more pissed I got. I couldn't even make the argument that we were dating because he couldn't afford to take me anywhere. And he was cool with that. After today, I wasn't settling for his mediocre lifestyle. It just wasn't enough for me.

Frustrated by sitting in my parking lot freezing my butt off instead of in the warmth of my office at work, I stepped out into the biting Chicago chill.

"I swear before the throne of God, if Ju has his tail in there laying on my good sheets and playing video games, I'm going to act a complete fool on him," I mumbled as I rubbed my arms.

When I entered the warmth of my apartment, I hurried through the living room and burst into my bedroom in a fury. And there he lay—all six feet of chocolate fineness splayed across my bed with a game controller resting comfortably in his big hands.

Just fine for no damn reason. He damn sure didn't know what to do with his fineness from nine to five.

"Bae, what you doing home?" he quickly sat up. "Shit, did Pam call you? She shouldn't have bothered you while you were working."

He had the nerve to say *I* shouldn't be bothered while *I* was working!

At this very moment, I didn't know what would be worse, coming home and finding him in bed with another woman or finding him lying here, playing games like a big kid.

I grasped my temples and rubbed them ferociously. "What am I doing home?" I asked. My pulse beat so loud I thought the thumping sound was a sure indication my heart was about to explode. "No, the question is, what the fuck are *you* doing home, Ju? Last time I checked, you had a job that you were supposed to be at today."

"Bae, calm down and let me explain," he said as he muted Dragon Quest with the hand controller, extinguishing the annoying noise blasting through the console.

I stood by the door with my shoulders rising and falling as I tried to calm down. I expected so much more from him, and he gave so little. I had a repulsion of spiders and flies. I'd lose my mind if one came near me. At the moment, Ju made me feel the same way about him. I watched him scramble to get out of bed and felt repulsed.

Ju walked over to me and attempted to upturn my face so I would look into his eyes.

I moved away from him. "Don't touch me. No, I'm not calming down. I had to put up with my boss' shit just to come home to check up on you like you're a toddler!"

"Bae, you didn't have to leave work. Everything is good."

"Why aren't you at work then? Why are you laying up in here chilling as if I work for the both of us? How do you plan to build anything with me when you can't even put in a day of work? Do you think I'm supposed to support you, Ju? Because if that is what you're thinking, you're wrong!"

He grabbed my hands and pulled me to him. "No, I don't think that. I just...I just want a better job. I don't like to work at that plant."

"Don't!" I pushed him away and glared into his honey brown eyes. "Don't give me any bullshit about how you don't want this work or that work."

He took a step toward me. "Kayla, listen."

I glared, daring him to approach me. "No, you listen. You've had at least ten jobs in the past few months, and you haven't made good on one of them. So to say that you want something better is just a lie. You have to start somewhere to get better. Nobody is looking for you while you're lying in your pajamas playing games. To get something, you're going to have to get up off your ass, get out of this apartment, and get it. Period."

"Kayla, will you just listen? Damn. All this attitude you're giving me is just unnecessary. What you're doing is pissing me off."

"Oh, great, you're pissed? It's amazing that you even think you have a reason to be pissed off. I want to hear this. Tell me why you are pissed, Ju!"

Ju sighed. "I'm pissed because you act like I'm not trying."

"You aren't trying, Jue, but it doesn't matter anymore. Just understand what I'm about to say because I'm about to piss you off even more. Since your actions have spoken for you, understand this..." I walked over to the closet and pulled down all of his neatly aligned Polo shirts. What unemployed man was lucky enough to have starched and pressed expensive shirts lined up, in every color, when they didn't have a job? Ju, that's who. I tossed each shirt down onto the floor, followed by the jeans I just had dry cleaned.

"Kayla, don't do that. You're messing up my dry cleaning."

"I want you and your stupid shirts out of here, now!"

He stormed over to me and used his strength to encircle me into his arms, the same arms that held me in place as he bewitched my body the night before. With a bear hug grip around me, he said, "You don't mean that, Kayla. I want to give you the world and I have been trying. You just don't give me credit for the things I do—"

"Like what?"

"Well, for one, keeping you satisfied."

"Oh, honey, you are mistaken. I wanted you for those things. I don't *need* you for them. I will be satisfied sexually one way or the other." I pushed him away with all the strength within me, causing him to loosen his grip on my arm. "You and me, we are done. I don't want you here anymore. All I want is for you to get out!"

A look of confusion covered his face. "I thought you loved me, Kayla."

"I did."

24

"You don't anymore?" he asked.

"The definition of love is sinking in and this is not it, Ju."

"Why're you doing this?"

"Just leave, please!"

I'd pleaded with him to do the right thing for a year. Now, the only plea I had left was for him to move on. The time had come for me to pick up the pieces of my life. I pointed to his clothes in the closet, letting him know he needed to start packing.

Finally, understanding his fate, he asked, "Where am I supposed to go? My family isn't gonna let me move in, and you know that. You're all I got, Kayla."

"You should've thought of that when you called out today. I told you last night that this would be the last straw. You should have believed me." I trekked to the kitchen to grab a big trash bag for his belongings. I hated that it'd come to this, but I refused to shoulder the burden for a whole human I didn't give birth to. Julius Johnson was *not* my child. "Go talk to your mother about moving in with her. I'm not her, though," I said when I walked back into the bedroom with the box of trash bags.

He sat on the bed, holding his head. He reluctantly took the trash bags out of my hand, walked over to the closet, and started stuffing his clothes in the bag.

I felt a pull at my heart when his pitiful-looking, light brown eyes collided with mine. I did have a lot of love for Ju, but he wasn't the man for me. I'd held on too long, hoping he would prove my parents wrong—it never happened.

Obviously, I wasn't the woman for him either. The right woman wouldn't have to ask him to build a life with her. He would happily work to support their dreams, simply because he wanted to.

An hour later, Ju walked to the door carrying his last bag over his shoulder. "I'm sorry, Kayla. I should've gone to work."

Yes, he should have, but it was too late to turn back now. "When you mature enough and find the right woman, it will all come together for you."

He pleaded with his eyes for me to give him a second chance. "I miss you already, Kayla."

"I'll miss you too," I said as a tear fell along my cheek.

"I will get it together and come back for you. You are the right woman, Kayla. You'll see," he promised. He dropped his bag from his shoulder and opened his arms for a parting hug.

I allowed myself to inhale the residue of his fresh mint body wash one last time. It felt right to rest against his firm muscles, and I clung to them for dear life. "Bye," I finally said and strolled over to the door. I held the door open for him to walk out.

He stopped at the top step. "Kayla?"

"Yeah?"

A pitiful look took over his handsome features. "Can you give me a jump?"

Ju having to ask for a jump start for his car was all the more reason we were done. What kind of man lays down when he has so many reasons to get up? If not for me, he should have gone to work to get a new battery—for himself.

"Sure," I said, turning to go get my keys. Strangely, it felt good knowing this would be my last time.

CHAPTER THREE

KAYLA

Should've Earned It

The next morning when I arrived at work, Helen stood in front of my desk, chatting with my colleague, Sandra Baxter. The two women talked about the weather and other mundane topics that dragged out Helen's time in our office. Undoubtedly, she was fishing for a way to bring up my leaving early yesterday, and it didn't take long for her to dangle the bait.

"Well, good morning Miss Kayla, so nice of you to join us again today," she said as if I were a repeat offender for truancy.

Not taking the bait, I smiled and said, "Good morning, Helen. Likewise."

She smiled deviously. "After the way you left yesterday, I didn't know if you'd be coming in today. Is everything okay?"

She had this nice-nasty way of pushing my buttons. What she said wasn't offensive; it was her attitude. It felt as if she was always trying to provoke me so that she could say, 'look at the only black woman in the office showing her black ass.' I refused to give her that satisfaction. "I'm ready for duty as always. How are you this morning, Helen? Sleep well? Oops, your ponytail is coming undone. Need a brush?" I asked. She wasn't the only one who could play nice-nasty.

"Oh, I slept very well," she said, smoothing down her hair. "Did you get your little problem handled at home? The darndest things keep happening to you."

"Yes, ma'am, I did. Thank you for being so gracious in allowing me to leave early. I don't know what I'd do without a wonderful boss like you. What do you say, boss of the year?" I raised a brow as if considering the idea. "What do you think, Sandra? Should we order the plaque now?"

A wide-eyed Sandra nodded. "Yeah, I think she should get boss of the year."

Helen pushed her chest out a little further, stepping away from my desk. "No, thanks ladies, but I should let you get to work. Seeing as how you neglected your evening duties yesterday, I'm sure you have a lot to do today, Kayla."

Looking over the notes I left in my daily planner, I said, "I'm on top of it, Helen."

She huffed and narrowed her brow as I made eye contact with her, then exited the room in a slumped stride.

Sandra covered her mouth to stifle her chuckles. "One of these days, the two of you are going to be rolling around on this carpet fighting. You get under each other's skin so bad."

I sat in my chair to put my purse and lunch bag away in my drawer. "I promise you that it's all her. As you know, I'm loveable." I shrugged my shoulders.

"You are loveable," Sandra agreed. "But when it comes to Helen, you turn into a different person."

Landing a media consultant position by the age of twenty-four took hard work. Four years later, I earned eighty thousand dollars a year. I wasn't about to let a miserable little woman like Helen knock me off my game. "If she'd just treat me like a human, life would be better for us all. You know she started a Helen-style argument about me leaving early?"

"I knew she would say something. But it was pretty quiet after you left, so it was nothing to worry about. One of your clients called and I left that message on your desk."

I picked up the note and read it. It was from Mr. Hammonds at TV One. "Cool, I'll give him a call back ASAP. I've been working with him to get those commercials set up for The Nullent Law Firm."

"Oh, that's going to be a good one."

"I know, honey. I can't wait to see that commission check. I rake good money into Naustram," I said as I snapped my fingers. "Jane Heard had better watch out because I'm coming for the number one spot."

Specializing in African American business to business promotions, I worked extremely hard for my clients. I was the second top producer at the company. Though Jane Heard worked with our mainstream account, which was code for top dollar white clients, I wasn't far behind her in sales. Intent on proving the power of the black dollar, I wanted to show I could be the top salesperson.

"I don't understand Helen's attitude toward you when you bring in so much money." Sandra shrugged. "It doesn't make sense." Sandra was a good person down to her very soul. She would give anyone the shirt off her back. She never said anything bad about anyone, always positive. So maybe she was just clueless to the evil lurking around her.

Helen had been prejudiced toward me, if not pure evil, but I'd dedicated too much mental space to her already, and it was barely 8:30 a.m. The only upside to my workplace drama would be the fact I hadn't thought about Ju since I'd arrived at work.

After crying him out of my system last night, I hoped not to hear from him again. I went on about my workday without too many distractions.

At lunchtime, my line buzzed. "Kayla Johnson speaking."

"Hey sis, I figured you'd need a pick me up after yesterday. I'm out here in the lobby. I came to take you to lunch."

Pam's cheerful voice was a refreshing interruption from the pile of work on my desk. I'd spoken with Mr. Hammonds and had been preparing a contract for two thirty-second commercials to run one thousand times over the next month on TV One's network for the Nullent firm. We agreed on a price, and I felt excited.

"Give me about five minutes," I told Pam, hung up, and finished the page I'd been reading. Our contracts were standard, but I wanted to make sure I didn't miss anything Mr. Nullent had specified to me.

After marking the page up with a highlighter, I put the document into a folder, picked up my purse, and looked at Sandra.

"Go on and eat lunch." She smiled at me. "I'll get the phones until you get back."

"Thank you. I won't be but an hour," I said.

I met Pam in the lobby, and we headed to Tanta's Restaurant.

Minutes later, I sat across from Pam in a booth, staring at the menu.

"Your man has been calling me all morning, trying to get me to put in a good word for him," Pam said, flipping through the menu pages. "He sounds desperate."

"Did you tell him to give it up?"

"I let him know that I stand with you. I told him to stop calling me and ended up blocking his number." Pam laughed. "He must not know I'm the one that told on him."

"I don't even care at this point. It's something about when you let a person go. That's when you see their true character for what it is. He's groveling now when all he had to do was go to work when he had me. How long did he think his joy ride would last?" I asked.

"I told you to dump him months ago, Kay."

"I know and you were right. I guess I was just caught up in helping him out. He was always saying he wanted to do better and how much he loved me."

She wiggled her brows. "You were caught up in something, alright."

"Okay, I agree that the sex didn't help the situation any. Whew, chile! I mean, you told me, my parents told me and hell...I even told myself. It's like a lightbulb went off and shined the light on him yesterday. I realized I was worth much more than he was giving."

"You *are* worth more. Ju didn't deserve you, my friend. You should be treated like a queen. At least that's what I want out of love," Pam said, her voice drifting away as she pushed a fluffy, jet black curl behind her ear.

"You sound like my parents now. My father is always telling me I need a man to treat me like a queen," I said, thinking of my father.

"It's the truth. That's why I'm single to this day. Men think I'm just supposed to give, give, give. What about me? I deserve something in return, or even to receive first," Pam fussed.

"Hey, we should start a self-love movement with a shopping spree. Do you want to do a little shopping with me out on Michigan Ave?" I waited for Pam's reply, and when she hesitated, I added, "I'll buy you something."

Excitement rushed over Pam's soft features then deflated. A sigh slipped past her glossy lips. My friend pouted, her long, twisted locks standing high on her head, making her look more naturally beautiful than ever. The rise and fall of her honey-colored cheeks followed by wrinkles forming on her forehead caused me to frown. "Man, I have to take my mother to the doctor at four. After we leave the doctor, she wants to go to her favorite soul food restaurant, so it'll probably be seven or eight before I'm free."

"Where are you guys going?" I asked.

"I wish Ronnie's was still open, but we're going to the suburbs to eat at Jessie's Diner," she said.

"Jessie's has good food. But have you been by Ronnie's lately? They've put up a *for sale* sign."

"Who are you kidding? I have the number programmed into my phone. All I'm waiting for is a bank to approve my business loan."

"Well, I hope you get it. I can't wait to eat at Pamelon's Soul Food."

She smiled and held up her hands in the prayer position. "From your mouth to God's ears."

"Yeah, well, now that Ju won't be around, I'm available to be used as your guinea pig for any new recipes you want to try."

"I'm trying a new mac' n cheese recipe tomorrow. I've added different cheeses and extra whipping cream."

My mouth watered at just the thought of this dish. "Your mac'n cheese can't get any better, so stop it!"

"That's not what your mother said when they visited last year."

"You can't judge anything by what my parents say. They are blunt about everything," I said.

"Well, at least I know where you get that trait from."

"I know, right. I'm just like them. But I'm not as blunt as my father; he doesn't care what he says or who he says it to." My phone vibrated, pulling my attention away. I reached into my purse to get it and immediately saw a text from Ju.

Ju: Hey

34

What do you want? I typed back.

My car broke down over on 21ˢᵗ Ave.

And? I asked. *Why are you telling me?*

I'm out here looking for work. Help a brother out.

Call Triple A, Ju. I dropped the phone back into my purse and stared off into the room, looking at no one or nothing in particular.

"Who was that?" Pam asked.

"It was Ju. He's broke down on 21ˢᵗ Ave."

"Girl, don't let him stress you out. His car may not even be broken down."

"I feel sorry for him, but I'm not going to help him," I admitted. "He has to find his own way from now on."

"And he will. Besides, he could just be trying to suck you back in."

"I know. I should text back and tell him to call the makers of Dragon Quest and see if they'll help him since he spent so much time and money on their products instead of working."

Pam laughed and held her hand up. "Exactly!"

I clapped her hand in sisterly agreement but felt a tug of war emerging inside of me. I wanted to help him. I also wanted to teach him a lesson. He had to do better. I turned my phone off and enjoyed lunch without the possibility of another intrusion.

CHAPTER FOUR

KAYLA

The Man in the Mirror

I strolled down Michigan Ave on this cool, crisp Chicago evening. It felt good to peek in the windows at the many extravagant material things the boutiques had to offer. A sudden chill caused me to snuggle up in my fur coat as I window shopped. The breeze tousled my hair, and my cheeks flushed. I breathed in the invigorating scent of fresh air and it gave me life as it caressed my skin with the artistry of a painter's brush.

I loved expensive things and while my income in media promotions was modest by some standards, I was good with money. I saved, invested, and from time to time, I treated myself to something nice. After taking responsibility for Ju for so long, it was time for me to spoil myself with something special. Every designer purse or high-end dress caught my eye.

The display in Jazzy Boutique's window stopped me mid-stroll. I stared at a black dress, clutch, and stiletto heels. I could just imagine being dressed in such a gorgeous outfit for a night on the town, my feet clinging sexily to the strapped heels. Just as I reached for the door, a brazen voice brought my shopping fantasies to a halt.

"Ma'am, I think you dropped this."

I caught the reflection of a handsome, elegantly dressed gentleman standing behind me. The mirror-like reflection bouncing off the store's door gave a clear view of his silky dark hair under the streetlights. His piercing blue eyes had a halting effect. He wore a custom suit worth thousands underneath an open trench coat. His gloved hand held my diamond earring. I'd saved three months for those earrings and almost lost one. I would have been distraught if I'd lost it.

When I turned to face him, my breath caught. Literally, I gasped. This man's reflection did him no justice. He was more handsome in the flesh. While I wasn't usually the nervous type, my gaze wandered away as I took my earring from his hand.

"Thank you," I muttered.

"You're welcome." A handsome grin crept onto the corners of his mouth. He seemed to enjoy my nervous reaction to him. "I know this is ridiculously presumptuous. But is there any chance you would like to go for a cup of coffee with me?" he asked, stopping me in my tracks as I was about to proceed into the boutique.

If I hadn't been certain nothing was behind me except a window full of mannequins, I would have checked over my shoulder to see what lucky woman this Adonis of a man was talking to. But since I was the only one standing there, I did the only thing that came to mind. I nodded dumbly.

Really Kayla?

I didn't nod when asked a question. Why was I doing it with this stranger?

I found my voice of reason and told him, "I mean, not today, but maybe we could meet at another time."

"Any time is fine with me." He smiled, showing off perfect teeth. An awkward moment passed between us before he pulled out a shiny business card and handed it to me. "You can reach me anytime at this number. Let my assistant know when you're ready and she'll have a car sent for you."

Assistant? Car sent? Not only was he working, but he also apparently had a good job. Kudo points were flowing in his favor. "Okay, will do," I said, taking his card.

"By the way, what's your name?" he asked.

I opened my mouth to speak. My throat felt awful dry, gritty even. My heart leaped as I froze for a second. Coughing to clear my throat, I said, "I'm—I'm Kayla."

"A beautiful name. Quite fitting..." He smiled, leaving the rest of the thought unsaid. "Nice to meet you, Kayla. I'm Rusty, and I look forward to seeing you again." He turned towards a limo parked behind him but then stopped and looked over at me. "Can I give you a lift anywhere?"

I shook my head and waved the handsome stranger away. I wasn't about to let him drop me off at my apartment on the Southside in a freaking limo. "No, thank you. I'll be fine. I drove myself here."

He scanned the area. There were no cars parked in front of the tolls. "Are you sure you don't need a ride? It wouldn't be a bother," he insisted.

"No, I'm very sure that I drove. Thank you."

"Okay. Have a great day, Kayla. I'll see you soon," he said with a nod. The chauffeur opened the door and Rusty disappeared inside.

I watched as the limo pulled off before I finally took a deep breath. My attention went to the business card in my hand. "My God, what just happened? Did a sexier than sexy white man driving a limo just try to get with me?" I asked aloud.

An older woman who stood nearby shrugged her shoulders. "You know, my dear, they say you start talking to yourself just before the mind slips away," she cackled.

"Yes, ma'am." Smiling, I turned on my heels and headed for the parking garage. Once in the car, I put his business card in my wallet. A man with a job was one step in the right direction.

CHAPTER FIVE

KAYLA

Self Love?

When I arrived at my apartment, Pam stood at the stove, stirring a large pot.

The entire place smelled of meat and spices. My stomach rumbled in the delight of the amazing aroma. With the window shopping, I'd worked up an appetite and nothing would be better right now than a dish of Pam's food. "Mmmm, what are you making?" I asked as I hung my coat in the front closet.

"Beef stew," Pam replied, glancing up from the pot. "I got home early from momma's appointment, so I decided to cook lunch for tomorrow. How was your shopping spree? I don't see any bags."

"Girl, I didn't see anything that I just had to have today," I said, though I did fall in love with an outfit hanging in Jazzy Boutique's window."

"Jazzy's? That place is so expensive."

"That's why I didn't buy the outfit today. If I still feel like I have to have it next week, I'll get it."

"Are you sure you're okay?" She walked over and touched the side of my head. "You don't feel warm or anything. It's not like you to come back empty-handed when you go shopping on Michigan Ave."

"Well, something interesting happened at Jazzy's." I dropped my purse down on the couch and let out a deep breath. "I met a guy."

"A guy?" Pam pushed long curls over her shoulder and gave me her undivided attention. "Don't you think it's a tad bit soon to meet a guy?"

I casually strolled over to the counter dividing the living room from the kitchen and sat down on one of the stools. "I just said I *met* a guy. I didn't say I was marrying a guy or about to move a guy in here. Besides, he probably could buy this apartment building and not miss the money from his account."

This piece of news caught Pam's attention. She leaned against the counter and stared at me intently. "Tell me everything. What's his name? What does he do? Is he handsome? When is your first date planned?"

"His name is Rusty, and according to his business card, he's the CEO of Digitek, Inc."

"Hmmm, interesting. I'm not familiar with the company, though."

"Well, according to Google, he's a successful social media developer. Starts up platforms similar to Snapchat, gets them popular, and then sells them."

She raised a brow. "So, you Googled him on the way home?"

41

"As soon as I got in the car. I wanted to know who I was talking to. Oh, and yeah, he wants to take me out for coffee."

Pam dropped the spoon into the pot and her hands went to her hips. "He's white, isn't he?"

My eyes widened and I tilted my head in surprise. "What makes you think that?"

"Well, for one, his name is Rusty. Two, he's a social media developer," Pam replied, scrutinizing me with her eyes. "Taking nothing from our brothers, they just usually are not tech geeks. Three, he asked you out for coffee. That's a pretty strong indicator that he's not a brother."

"Brothers drink coffee." I shifted in my chair. "And what if he is white?"

She cut her eyes at me. "When a white man goes after a black woman, they are usually up to no good, so you shouldn't trust him one bit!" she sniped.

"Huh? What in the hell is that supposed to mean? According to your logic, black women are no good since white men going after us makes them no good," I said, trying to make sense of her racial ideology that caught me by surprise.

"Twist my words if you want," she snapped. "You said this guy is rich, right? And he can't even take you out for dinner? All you get is a cup of coffee. And I bet before the cup is half empty, he's going to want to take you to a motel. And you're going to be so flattered that a white man even looked your way that you're going to give up the booty to a man who didn't even think it was worth a steak dinner. He probably just has a bit of jungle fever that he wants to play out, and then he'll dump your black ass."

My mouth fell open as I bristled. "Whoa, what's your problem?"

"I don't have a problem, except I know firsthand how it works."

"So, are you saying you dated a white man before?"

"Actually, I have, and it's nothing I care to talk about. Just remember my words to you on this. I'm telling you from experience. They get what they want from you, then go off with their white friends like they never even knew you."

"Well, rest assured that you don't have to worry about me giving it up to the first man to hand me a cup of coffee, no matter what color he is, even though I think he's a good guy," I said, wondering why I was defending a man I hardly knew. After Ju, I should be running away from all mating prospects.

Pam had some pretty strong opinions about love...or pretty much everything, but to suggest that I would be interested in a man for no other reason than his race and money was a low blow. I judged men on their merit, not their color or riches. Her being my friend, she should know this, but something had left a sore spot on her beautiful soul. It left me staring at her and wondering, "Who hurt you?"

"That's not the point," she said. "I just thought we were about to head into a self-love phase where we didn't put men at the top of our priority list. Just when I get my mind wrapped around the whole idea, you come home talking about dating someone."

"Apology accepted. But I don't have a big 'D' on my forehead for 'Dumbo.' Do you think I would just allow myself to be used up again? It's just coffee. Not a real date."

Pam's intense expression softened. She walked over to me and wrapped her arms around me. "Forgive me, best friend. I know what I said was rude, but I only want to look out for you. Just be careful with this man, okay?"

"Okay." I clutched my best friend's arm. "I know you're looking out for me. But don't worry. I'm a big girl, and I can take care of myself. I may get caught up in love's cloud. But trust me, the fog always clears. And when it does, I can see things clearly."

"I just feel like I need to protect you." Pam released me and walked back over to the stove. She stirred the pot one more time and cut off the fire. "Dinner should be cool enough to eat in about twenty minutes."

"Cool, and thanks."

She nodded at me.

I headed to my room. I pulled off my confining dress suit, showered, and put on a long t-shirt and yoga pants. I sat on the edge of my bed, legs crossed and took out the business card Rusty had given me.

A business card was a bit impersonal, wasn't it? Shouldn't he have given me his private line if he was serious about seeing me again? What if Pam was right and he wanted to use me to fulfill some sort of colorful fetish?

With too much to consider, I decided just to avoid calling him at all. He didn't have my number or even know my last name. If I never called, then this would all be over before it started. That way, I was safe from another potential heartbreak. I threw the card on the dresser and laid down on my empty bed. I felt so exhausted from the long day that it wasn't long before sleep overpowered me.

CHAPTER SIX

Kayla

Care to Add a Little Cream?

Two weeks after throwing Ju out, my life was getting back to a semblance of normalcy. I wasn't crying my eyes out at night, missing him holding me or talking to me about my day. I walked around in my yoga pants and a long tee-shirt on Saturdays and Sundays, but I wasn't doing any yoga unless you counted the acrobatic way I lifted my spoon to my mouth to stuff it with more of Pam's famous chili. I wholeheartedly believed one day she would open a restaurant like she always dreamed, and when she did, customers were going to flock to it for her delicious dishes.

Lifting my hand to take one more bite of the chili allowed me to get a whiff of the stale odor coming from underneath my arms. "That's it... I'm at least going to shower and get dressed," I said.

A Saturday night and I hadn't changed clothes since I got off work Friday evening. I went into my room and opened the closet. I picked out a chocolate brown dress that had a pink belt and matching pink shoes. After laying them out on the bed, I went into the closet to find my pink scarf.

Pulling it down from the top of the closet, one of Ju's ties fell at my feet. Hoping the fabric would have a trace of his scent, I bent over to pick it up and instinctively brought it to my nose. I wanted to remember the man I fell in love with—the one I gave a year of my life to. Regardless of why we split, I did care about him and still wanted the best for him.

Snapping out of it, I tossed the tie into the trash bin. He was gone for a reason.

I went into the bathroom and turned on the shower. When it got warm enough, I stepped into the steamy shower and reveled in the refreshing feel of the water beating down my breasts, stomach, and thighs. I grabbed my lavender bath gel and squeezed an ample amount onto the loofah before scrubbing my body. When the fragrant smell of lavender perfumed every inch of my skin, I turned the shower off and stepped out. It always seemed incredible how something as simple as a shower could change the whole world.

After drying off, I stepped into a pair of pink lace panties. I walked over to my dresser to find my lotion and an envelope fell to the floor. I picked it up, and underneath it was Rusty's card. I threw the card and envelope back onto my dresser. Something made me pick the card up again and stare at it the same way I had the first day I met him.

He's so cute.

And charming.

And sexy as hell.

I'd been sitting around, spending my free time moping over my failed relationship with Ju. Meanwhile, Rusty had probably forgotten me after two weeks passed by without hearing from me. At this point, what could I do about his offer to take me for coffee? The answer was simple... I'd move forward and call him Monday. I'd find out what the deal was with him and, at the same time, be cautious. I finished getting dressed and left the house to catch a late movie with my plan in mind.

*

"It's a great day at Digitek. You've reached Rusty von Strauss' office. This is Cassandra speaking. How may I help you?" a chipper voice spoke to me. It was 10 a.m. Monday morning, and I'd called the number on Rusty's card.

"Hi Cassandra, this is Kayla Johnson. I'm calling to schedule a meeting with Mr. von Strauss."

Just before calling him, I'd looked up his Facebook profile. It was private—only his friends could see the things he posted on there. However, his company profile was booming with new happenings, innovative ideas, and product launches.

"Of course, Ms. Johnson. Mr. von Strauss has been expecting your call. Coffee, correct? How about today at 2 p.m.?" she asked but didn't give me time to answer. "There is a quaint little coffee shop on the corner of Michigan and Lake that he would like to take you."

"Really? Today? Yeah, I mean, yes. That's only a couple of blocks from here...Sounds great," I said, smiling at her confirmation that Rusty had been expecting my call.

"Great, I will let Mr. von Strauss know. Do you want a car to come to get you?" she asked.

I smiled. "No, I won't need a ride, but thanks."

"Okay, your meeting is set for today at two p.m. Just to be sure that you have all the details, I will text them to the number you called. Is that a good number for you to receive texts?" she chirped.

"Yes, it is. Thanks."

"You're welcome!"

I hung up and pushed back my lunch meeting to later in the afternoon. The place he wanted to meet was only a few blocks away, which was a plus.

After I scheduled our coffee date, time seemed to stop moving. Every time I glanced at the clock, sure that at least twenty minutes had passed, I found it had been more like five. My stomach felt like it was in a spin cycle as I waited for the time for the coffee date to arrive.

Why did I feel so nervous? He's just a guy I met. We're just having coffee. Still, the wait until two seemed unbearable. I could hardly focus on work.

At 1:50 p.m., I headed for the door. I walked the two blocks to the coffee shop in no time but stopped in my tracks when I reached it.

The place was empty and there was a closed sign on the door. I stared owlishly at the black sign printed in bold white letters. It was the middle of the day on a Thursday. No way should it be closed.

As I pondered what was going on, a barista walked up to the front door and opened it. "Ms. Johnson?" he asked skeptically.

I nodded in complete confusion.

He stepped back, holding the door open for me. "Please come in."

I entered cautiously like I expected the doors to slam shut and suck me into a black hole at any moment. Everything looked the same as I recalled from the last time I'd been here. Multi-colored ceramic cups littered the walls. Brightly painted, used, mismatched furniture was strewn throughout the space.

The young man in his green polo shirt stepped behind the counter and asked, "What can I get for you?"

"Um, where is everyone?" I asked. This shop was never this empty. I felt like I'd jumped into some sort of crazy ghost film.

The young man opened his mouth to answer and the door chimed.

I turned just in time to see Rusty entering. The air grew thick and my breath caught. If I thought he looked handsome the first time I saw him, he looked even more so this time. I couldn't put my finger on exactly why. He wore another shamefully expensive suit with a light blue silk shirt and a dark, solid blue tie. He breezed in with the same swagger of confidence that made me swoon the first time.

When his gaze met mine, he took off his sunglasses and smiled wide. His teeth glistened like he should have been a model for a Colgate commercial. "How are you?" he asked.

Good, now that you're here. "I'm well. And you?" I asked, sure my smile reflected his.

"Good. Did you order yet?"

"I was just about to." I turned back to the barista and said, "Caramel macchiato."

Rusty didn't place an order.

The barista quickly handed him a cup and said, "Coffee black, sir." He then gave me my drink.

We took our drinks and sat at one of the tables.

I looked around at the empty room and said, "This is really creepy, isn't it?"

Rusty scanned the room. "What is?"

"That we're the only people here in the middle of the day. That's so weird, don't you think?"

"Oh, that. I bought the space for our date. I hate to try to get to know someone with other people making noise in the background. I don't want to miss anything that you have to say."

Blood rushed to my cheeks. His charm disarmed me in every possible way. His looks. His scent. His thoughtfulness. I'd have to be careful not to fall into the tangled web of the charming tech mogul. *You're not the first girl he shut down a restaurant for,* I nudged myself.

Sitting across the table from him peering into his eyes, I figured if a girl were to get caught up with Rusty, she'd probably never get out of his hold. I squared my shoulders, summoning every bit of my resolve from deep within. "That's a bit extravagant, isn't it?"

He flashed a wickedly sexy grin. "It's just a coffee shop. An afternoon wasn't that expensive," he said as if he were talking about buying a stick of gum.

Pam's remarks about him taking me on a cheap date came to mind. "Why coffee? Why not by out a restaurant for dinner or take me to a date to the theater?" I didn't know why I asked this. I guess I wanted to tell Pam something when I saw her again.

"Isn't this what all the blogs suggest? It's low pressure. It's quiet so that we can talk. It can be as long or as short as we want to make it. If you decide you don't like me, you can finish off your coffee and head out. With dinner, you'd run the risk of spending all evening getting dressed in your best clothes, makeup, hair...only to find out you don't like me after all."

I snickered. "And what if you decide that you don't like me?"

"Do that again."

"What?"

"That."

I had no idea what he was talking about, so I just stared.

The dreamiest smile crept upon the corners of his lips. "Has anyone ever told you how gorgeous you are, Kayla?"

I lifted my cappuccino and stared at him over the rim of my cup. My heart kept doing summersaults in my chest as I took a sip. I watched his lips move, but the words came out in slow motion.

"I don't think that it's possible not to like you," he continued when I didn't answer his question. "Can I confess something here?"

I nodded. "Sure." Who was going to stop him?

"Work keeps me very busy, so I don't have much time for meaningless dates. I don't take women out to places to hear them talk if you get what I'm saying. But with you, I'm just trying to make it through the next twenty or so minutes without looking like a total ass so that you'll be willing to go out with me again."

I sat my cup down and offered a genuine smile. "Don't worry. You're doing an excellent job so far."

"I'm glad to hear that. So what should we talk about first?" he asked.

I wanted to know, "What made you ask me out?"

"I was hoping the inside was as lovely as the outside and so far, I haven't been disappointed." He seemed to always know what to say. It was adorable.

As we drank our coffee, we talked about our careers, which later turned into a discussion on movies and, after that, music.

By the time I glanced down at my watch, it was thirty minutes past time for me to leave. "Oh, no!" I jumped up from the table, hauling my purse onto my shoulder. "I need to get back to work. My boss is probably circling my desk like a piranha."

Rusty stood from his seat. "Can I see you for dinner tomorrow?"

"Uh," I hesitated. "Tomorrow?"

"If not tomorrow, when is good for you?" he asked with an intense glimmer in his blue eyes.

Handsome, adorable, and easy to talk to. I couldn't say I'd blame a girl for hopping inside his limo and bending to his will. He probably was playing a little cat and mouse game with me until I did just that.

Looking around at the empty coffee shop, I said, "This was nice, but I want a nice dinner date next time."

Rusty nodded curtly. "If that's what you want, that's what you'll get. I'll show you a night you won't forget."

I took a deep breath, considering his offer. I pulled out a scrap of paper and wrote down my number.

He immediately punched the numbers into his phone and sent me a text. "I just sent you my private line, Kayla. Only a select few people have that number, so guard it with your life," he said jokingly.

Truth or not, it certainly made me smile.

"What's your address? I may surprise you," he asked.

"No surprises," I said, wondering if he'd still be interested in me once he pulled his fancy limo up to my address. It wasn't the worst neighborhood, but I'd been saving to buy a better place.

He handed me his phone. "Type it in."

I defiantly stared into his smoldering, ocean blue eyes. His voyeuristic gaze sent a tingle through my body. "What if I say no?"

"You won't," he replied.

And he was right. A force of nature had my fingers typing in the details. "Call before you come over," I said in an attempt to exhibit some bit of control.

"I'll be seeing you soon."

"Okay. I have to go now," I said with anxiety riddling inside me. Soon, I would be back in my office and at Helen's mercy. "Talk to you soon," I said and turned toward the door.

Rusty drew me into his arms for a lingering hug. My breasts pressed against his chest and his woodsy cologne impaled my senses. It was an innocent embrace. Yet, it became a part of me I didn't want to let go of. My eyes collided with his as I slipped out of his arms and took a step backward, leaving the shop. A hug from a virtual stranger wasn't supposed to elicit this type of response.

Once outside, I rushed the two blocks over to the office as fast as I could. If anyone noticed I was thirty minutes late from break, no one said anything. I went back to my desk and began the tedious work of daydreaming of Rusty's smile, laugh, and the hug that still embraced me.

CHAPTER SEVEN

RUSTY

All That Glitters Ain't Gold

My daily schedule had become unusually humdrum. Jog. Work. Home. More work. Sleep. Occasionally, an unattached, nameless rendezvous thrown into the mix, but I hadn't even been doing that lately. Day after day, I did the same thing all over again. I didn't feel bad about working long, hard, mind-numbing hours because it had been those long nights and hard days that brought my fortune.

"That will be all, Wendell. I'm staying in the rest of the night," I said to my driver as he pulled up to my penthouse. He knew my routine, so I wasn't sure why I announced it. Maybe to cement staying in tonight into reality.

"Good evening, sir. Same time, same place at seven a.m.?"

Wendell's voice cut through my thoughts as I sat in the back seat, peering up at my living room window. The idea of spending an evening in solitude engulfed me. "Change of plans. Come back in two hours. I'm going out," I said as I stepped out and closed the door.

"Yes, sir. I will be here in exactly two hours."

"Thanks." I watched Wendell whisk around the lot and drive to the exit. The limo disappeared around the corner as I made it up the walkway to my penthouse. I stared up at the tall building. My abode was on the top floor. The entire top floor.

A smile crept upon the corners of my lips as I looked at what I'd done. The life I created was a long shot from the slumlords and my mother's tears over not giving me a better life. May my sweet mother, Anna von Strauss, preceded in death by my hard-working father, Lawrence von Strauss, rest in peace. Because of them, I could afford the greatest things this life could provide. The drive they instilled in me had been the reason I worked harder than any kid from our neighborhood. I strived to be the best at everything I did. I wanted the best. I tried to put to use everything they taught me. I only wished they were alive to share it with me.

A downside of my success was that it made me a walking magnet. All sorts of people, good and bad, wanted to attach themselves to me. Women worked tirelessly to sink their claws into me.

The day before I met Kayla, a bewildered woman threw her panties into my rolled-down window. I didn't even know her name or where she came from. I growled and tossed her panties out onto the street. After threatening to call the police if she ever pulled a stunt like that again, I told Wendell to drive off.

Memories of a time when my love life was much better flooded my mind. I missed Paula. Our favorite song,

There will never be another you came to mind, but I pushed the thought aside quickly... too painful to think of her.

There weren't many genuine people left. In the wake of my booming success, women were eager to get into my bank account. Pretending to want me was the pretense. Paula never treated me like a money machine. She genuinely loved me. Since her passing, the choice to have only one night stands had been an easy one to make. I didn't want any attachments.

I gave up on finding true love again. I only dated to soothe my desires if you could call that dating. To be truthful, it was more like wining and dining to get to the bedroom to relieve sexual tension.

Perplexingly, I hadn't entertained a woman at my home since I met Kayla. I blamed my seclusion on my busy schedule. But I really couldn't get her beauty out of my mind.

Wendell and Cassandra took turns teasing me about my suddenly stagnant social life. "You're becoming such a recluse...all work and no play is never good," they'd said to me in different ways.

Regularly, I thought of the coffee date with Kayla. I wanted to get to know her better. I should've forgotten about her and continued having empty conversations and meaningless sex with random women. It was safer than putting my heart on the line again.

I thought about calling up a warm body and making it an entertaining evening. It sounded good in theory, except I could only think of Kayla. I had to see her again.

"How are you this evening?" I asked the front desk attendant as I passed through the entranceway.

"Better, now that you're here," she said, showing a glimpse of a sparkling, toothy smile.

"Have a great day, Mrs. Terrell."

"You too, Mr. von Strauss. Buzz down if you need anything."

I nodded.

"And I do mean *anything...*" she repeated with a devious wink of her long lashes.

"Goodbye, Mrs. Terrell." Shaking my head, I pressed the button for my floor. I soon entered my penthouse apartment. Floor to ceiling windows greeted me with the beauty of sunset all around me.

The living room, designed by the best damn home interior designer in Chicago, welcomed me back. The regal blend of white and beige pulled me in, comforting me immediately. I sank into the sofa and stared off into space.

My long day soaked in. I felt on edge. The deals, the wheels, the nuts and bolts of my business were high on my mind. Those thoughts only being invaded by the window-shopping ebony queen I'd shared coffee with earlier today. Perhaps one night with her would be enough to get her out of my system.

Yes, indeed. That was it. One night with the ebony beauty. One and done.

I picked up my cell phone and scrolled through numbers until I found Kayla Johnson. I dialed her number.

She picked up on the first ring. "Hello," her melodic voice sang into the phone.

"Hey, Kayla," I began. "I was calling to see—"

"Rusty?" she cut me off. "Hey, I didn't expect you to call tonight." A smile entered her voice.

I was hoping she'd be happy to hear from me. "Yes, I'm sorry I'm calling so soon. I just couldn't wait."

"No, you're fine. Just good to know you haven't forgotten me already." She giggled, and even her laughter was sexy.

"No, never." It was impossible to control my delight of hearing her voice as I sat there, smiling like a Cheshire cat.

"Well, that's good to know." Her tone became more serious. "What can I do for you?"

"Be dressed and ready to go in an hour. I'm coming over to fetch you."

"Fetch me? Excuse me?" Her tone went from nervously sweet to questioning.

"I'm coming to get you, Kayla, so wear something nice. Text me your address again because it didn't save when you entered it into my phone." I hung up before she could object.

A rush ran through me as I stood up and walked to my bedroom to get dressed. When my phone rang a few minutes later, I smiled. Didn't she know our date was non-negotiable? "Are you getting ready, darling? And don't forget to text me—"

"I need you, Rusty!" The grating sound of a desperate voice shrieked in my ear.

Recognizing the voice, my stomach churned. "Meagan, why are you calling me?"

She sniffled. "I can't live without you, Rusty, please!" A full blow from her nostrils sounded off on the phone, making my stomach bubble over more with disgust. "Please, listen to me."

"Meagan, we've been over this before," I said, sick of explaining to her why we just would never work. The reason should not have been hard for her to understand. I blew out a sigh to release the building tension from my body.

"Please, help me understand how you could just break things off after all we shared?"

I ran my fingers through my hair and sighed. Every few months, Meagan had a breakdown like this and called me crying. I despised when these nostalgic moments brought her to this state. Had I known it was her calling and not Kayla, I would not have answered.

"Rusty, talk to me. Tell me why you don't want me anymore," she whined.

"Meagan, stop playing the victim. You know damn well why we aren't together. I didn't just up and break things off with you. We wanted different things out of the relationship. I wanted to love you, and you wanted my money. I'm not a person to hold on to something that's not working." Hopefully, she would understand my thousandth explanation as to why I broke things off with her.

It had become painfully obvious when money went missing from my account and appeared in hers that Meagan wanted a bank and not a soulmate. The way she misused my trust had ruined me for other women.

"I don't want anyone but you, Rusty. All I want is you. I need you. We work!" she hollered her feelings into the phone. "I gave you all of me, and you left me. If you would just try to understand."

"You have to stop calling me about this, Meagan. Get a grip and be honest with yourself, for once. We haven't been together in over a year. I have moved on. You should too."

She started coughing and snorting into the phone like she had a violent anoxic attack. I became worried she would need medical help until she said, "You've moved on? But we were supposed to get married. I picked out my colors and everything. I told my family we were going to get married."

"You know what you did to me, Meagan," I reminded her. "I don't understand why you insist on playing the victim. It is time to move on."

"We were the power couple of Chicago," she continued, ignoring everything I said to her. "Why can't you give us another chance?"

She was right. To the public eye, we were perfect. She doted on me and acted as if I were her beginning and end. I whisked her in and out of my limo as if she were precious, fragile cargo whenever we arrived at events. Turned out to be a huge sham.

I'd been working hard to build a new life with my new lover and newfound fortune. Then every chance Meagan got, she would be transferring money into her private bank account. She'd been so conniving that she used my hard-earned money to fund her father's technology business, which grew so fast by using my cash that he became my competitor.

"Meagan, what we had is in the past. It's time for you to stop holding on."

"Rusty, please don't hang up. Come over to my place. Better yet, I'll come to you. Like I told you before, I'll replace the money, every dime of it. Just give me an hour of your time, and let me make you forget every single thing I've ever done wrong."

"No, no, I'm not coming over there and please don't come here. You will just be wasting your time."

She gave another loud sniffle, then lowered her voice. "Please, baby, please. Give me one more chance to make it up to you. I can make you forget about the past."

"Don't lower yourself to begging because the answer is no, forever. I don't care how much you cry or what you propose to do for me. We are done!" I hated to be callous, but I had to talk to her bluntly without sugar-coating it for her to get the point. She still ran the risk of missing the point.

"But, Rusty."

"No buts, I don't have time to spare on this type of stress. I have plans for this evening."

"Why are you treating me like this, Russ? Who is she?" she asked.

I let out a loud sigh and said, "Goodbye." I ended the call and immediately blocked Meagan's new number. Her betrayal was the main reason I stayed single—too many opportunistic people in this world.

When I first met Meagan, I'd been in a rebirth period in my life. Paula had just divorced me, and I was determined to start over with a fresh slate. I promised Paula I would move on, and I wanted to make good on it.

After making one of the most challenging decisions in my life, I put my heartache aside and pummeled my way into the social engineering machine as an entrepreneur. All work and no play, I kept my mind off my personal life, which was in shambles. Meagan came along and introduced me to the socialite life. I welcomed the sexy vixen who was a mixture of sweet, knowledgeable, and did I mention sexy? She seemed to be the perfect fit for me. Sometimes, she even helped me forget about the huge cloud hanging over my head.

While I fought my way to the top, Meagan was born into money. Her keen knowledge of the finer things in life intrigued me. Her kindness was charismatic to my soul. Our romantic relationship burned like an ember we both took turns stoking. It would've lasted until the end of time had that five hundred thousand dollars never gone missing from my bank account, proving that every thought I had of her had been a farce.

I'd been going over my reports one Saturday morning trying to figure out where I was misspending, and *boom*, the discrepancy hit me like a boulder. Meagan's big smile that had once lit a fire inside me had also smothered me with darkness.

"What the hell?" I said when I saw a Bill Pay transfer for nine thousand dollars drafted from my savings account. I continued scrolling and caught another and another, all for nine thousand. "Meagan..." I said when I called her number, though still not believing that she'd done it.

"Hello," she answered my call on the first ring. "Before you say anything, sweetheart, you won't believe the sales out here today. I know you always talk to me about being better with spending, so you will be proud of me for saving money."

"Ironically, money is the reason I called you."

She paused before asking, "What's wrong?"

"I don't know. Maybe you can tell me why I'm missing four hundred ninety thousand dollars from my savings account? And before you say anything, please know that I know the answer to that question."

"Rusty, honey, I was going to tell you about it. I used the money that I was supposed to renovate my house with and let my father borrow it. He lost millions in the market and told me he only needed a few hundred thousand to get his business back going."

A few hundred thousand? We were talking about a half a million dollars!

"I never intended for you to spend a half-million dollars on your fucking house, and even if I did, you just took the good deed I was doing for you and gave my money to your father without informing me about it?" It was a question, but more so, I realized what happened to my money as I spoke. I had been played.

Her tone lowered when she replied, "I should have asked you, yes, but I planned to get it back before the end of the month. It was supposed to be there before you did your books."

"But you didn't get it back in my account, and the fact that you tried to hide this from me is even worse than you lending your father my money." Her father was now a competitor in the same market while running an aggressive advertisement program that pulled my customers to his business. Now, I knew how it was being financed.

"I know Rusty and I feel awful," she said in a whining tone.

My money was missing and she was out shopping. Yet, she felt awful? I didn't think so. "I tell you what, Meagan. You can keep the money. Don't worry about paying me back. Keep it as a parting gift. It's over."

"Rusty—" she hummed out before I hung up the phone and slammed the top down on my laptop.

When I found out Meagan stole money from me, I didn't know what to think about finding someone to love. I'd let my guard down for a vulture and dared not to do it again. I wanted no part of Meagan's deceptiveness, especially after experiencing the most genuine love from the sweetest soul alive. Paula would have never treated me like that. Damn, I missed her.

I didn't know what it would take to get it through Meagan's thick skull that it was over. I tossed my phone down on the bed and stepped into my adjourning bedroom closet to find something casual to wear for the evening. Meagan's call had put me in an angry mood. Hearing from her brought a spirit of precaution and hung it over Kayla's bright smile and sweet essence. As much light as I saw in her big brown eyes at our coffee date, I had to beware. All that glittered wasn't gold, especially when it came to women.

CHAPTER EIGHT

KAYLA

A Shondaland Type of Night

It was my turn to cook, so I went into the kitchen to make dinner after work. I wanted to get everything ready before six, so I could relax and watch my favorite TV show, *Scandal*, at eight.

Halfway through a delicious meal of oven-fried chicken, steamed asparagus, and baked potatoes, Pam showed up, kicked off her shoes, and plopped down on the couch. "You won't believe what this banker had the nerve to say to me today," she sighed.

"Huh, what did you say?" I asked softly. The wistfulness of a woman riding the high of an unexpectedly great coffee date could be heard in my voice. If I could hear it, Pam caught it too.

"He said something stupid about the loan for the restaurant, but who cares? Did you see that rich white guy again?"

I giggled and covered my mouth as I spoke, "Yeah, we went for that coffee we were talking about."

"I take it you enjoyed sipping coffee with the rich and famous. Tell me everything. How was he to talk to? Are you guys going on another date, Kayla? What's the deal?" Pam shot off rapid-fire questions.

"He is so less complicated than I thought he would be. I enjoyed having coffee with him. So much so that I was thirty minutes late getting back from my lunch break, and you know how Helen is about that."

"The conversation had to be good to keep you thirty minutes over," she said with a smirk.

I smiled. "I had no concept of time when I was with him."

"Oh, my. Well, as much smack as I talked before, he may turn out to be a good one." She walked over to peek into the oven. "Are the potatoes ready? I'm starving," she asked, rubbing her stomach.

"They have about fifteen more minutes," I said, looking at the timer. "Speaking of talking smack. When I told you about Rusty, you mentioned someone from your past. What did you mean by that?"

Her eyes dimmed as her shoulders slumped. "Oh, just a guy I fell in love with in high school."

"Just a guy you fell in love with? What?"

"Yeah, believe it or not, we had a full-blown love affair going on, but it turned out to be one-sided. Actually, to this day, I think that he loved me too; he just didn't want to come out and tell people about us. His parents were staunchly against us being together, and he was afraid to tell his friends, but he didn't have a problem with sneaking in my window late at night or kissing me in an empty band room."

"Too bad for him. It's sad to love someone and not show it because you're worried about what everyone else will say, think, or do."

"Well, that was Lyle Walker. He obviously worried more about what people said than what his own heart spoke to him. And when you told me about Rusty, everything I experienced with Lyle came back, from the beginning to the end, when he broke my heart in front of a gymnasium full of people."

"It's his loss." Lyle sounded like a loser to me.

"Yeah, when his friend asked him why that 'black chick' was following him around, everything went to shit," she admitted.

"Wow, what did he say to him?"

"He looked at me like I was a fly buzzing around his ear and said, 'I dunno what's wrong with her, dude.' He denied me in front of all those people standing in the gym, and I haven't forgiven him for the way that made me feel."

"Did you haul off and slap him?" I asked, knowing the Pam I knew would've kicked his ass.

"No, I tucked my head between my tail and called my mom and asked her to check me out of school. Later that night, I heard a tap on my window. It was Lyle trying to get in. Standing on the other side of my windowpane, a nonverbal apology was in his eyes. That was when I opened the window and doused him with a bucket of ice-cold

70

water. I had it waiting just in case he was dumb enough to show up."

"You know what, he probably loved you. He just wasn't bold enough to handle what people thought of him dating you at his young age. Just out of curiosity, is he still in Chicago, or did he move away?"

"I didn't keep track of him after I graduated from college. After that night, I dodged him like he dodged me before. Once I started to ignore him, he didn't care who knew how he felt. He started chasing me, not caring who saw his attempts to kiss up to me."

"You got back together?" I asked.

"For a while in college, but he still wasn't comfortable with our relationship, so I let go. I changed my number, moved out of my apartment, and stopped talking to our mutual friends. I did everything so he wouldn't be able to contact me again."

"Do you think he really cared about you?" I asked more out of curiosity of what Pam thought. I could see how much she cared about him in her eyes.

"It didn't matter to me at that point." She shrugged her shoulders.

"Well, it's a damn shame he didn't figure out how much he cared about you until it was too late. I'm surprised he hasn't found you and apologized."

"I don't want an apology, so enough about that." Pam forced a smile, though this was obviously a sore spot for her. "Let's just hope Rusty is nothing like Lyle."

"I'm not putting too much hope into anything beyond a date. He said he wanted to take me out soon, and that's where we left it off."

"Just take it one step at a time, Kayla. He wants to take you out on a real date. At least, he's moving in the right direction."

I chuckled. "Coffee and conversation is a real date. And wouldn't you know, I made it through that date with only exchanging a hug. I didn't blow him in the back of his limo or anything like you suggested would happen."

Pam looked apologetic. "I knew you wouldn't do that. I said those things out of my own hurt, and I'm sorry."

"Well, I accept your apology. I must say, Rusty left a lasting impression on me. He's sweet. And funny. And so down to earth. You'd think a guy like that wouldn't be. That he'd be stuck up, but he's not. I'll admit, he has the quirks that make him adorable." I smiled, thinking about Rusty's personality.

"Quirks. What kind of quirks?" Pam asked.

"Like, even though he's thought of as outgoing, he's really an introvert. You'd think with all the business he does that he'd be an extrovert. But he had the entire coffee shop cleared out just so he wouldn't have to deal with others making noise."

"Oh, so he paid for the building, so you could have coffee alone?"

"Yep."

Pam low-key hinted at his motive when she said, "So, no one else was there during your coffee date? Just you two, secluded and out of the public eye?"

"Wait, I don't think he was trying to hide anything," I defended. "He just wanted an intimate setting."

Pam tilted her head to the side and nonchalantly said, "Uh-huh."

Rusty gave off good vibes, but after Ju, I couldn't trust a man unless he proved himself to be worthy of my trust. I felt thankful for Pam's hints that made me think deeper about Rusty's actions. Staring into her intense eyes, I said, "No need to worry, my friend. He's going to call to set up another date, and I will see how it turns out. Whatever happens, happens."

She raised her hand in the air and splayed two fingers out. "If he doesn't call, fudge him. Two fingers in the air, deuces."

I smiled. "I know, right?"

"Well, I just want to say that it's great seeing you flaunt around here, smiling again. Just be careful with this guy, Kay."

"I will, but he might just be the way," I said.

Pam shook her head. "You're a hopeless romantic. Have you ever met a man that you didn't think was 'the one' in the beginning?"

I shook my head. "No. I haven't."

We broke out into laughter.

The time I spent with Rusty at the coffee shop was different from the time I'd spent with any other man, but she was right. I wondered if a romantic date with Rusty would be the best thing for me. The last thing I wanted was to become a sap for a man who was just looking for a fling. Maybe it'd be a good thing if he didn't call. It'd give me time to refocus on what's important, which was being happy— with or without a man.

While I quickly finished up dinner, Pam went to take a shower. I was just about to set the table when my phone rang. I sighed before answering the unknown number, "Hello?"

"Hi, Kayla," he began. "I was calling to see if you—"

"Oh, hey, Rusty?" I asked in surprise. "I didn't expect you to call tonight."

"Yes, I'm sorry I'm calling so soon. It's just that—"

"No, you're fine. Just glad you haven't forgotten about me already," I answered with a giggle.

Rusty informed me he was on his way to pick me up for a date and it was non-negotiable. He said he was coming to "fetch" me. Reserved and excited, he hung up before I actually agreed to go out with him.

I stood there, listening to the dead air on the phone line. He had some nerve to think I would up and go out on a date with him with a few minutes' notice. I huffed.

I can't believe this!

Didn't he know a woman had to make preparations? Hair? Attire? Nails?

I picked up the plate from the kitchen table to take back to my bedroom. I came up with my rebuttal as I listened to the swishing of the fish tank. When I finished my dinner, I would call and ask for a raincheck. "I'm not some desperate woman sitting around here eating alone, waiting for a TV show to give me my once a week entertainment." I definitely was, but he didn't have to know that.

I bit down on a piece of asparagus that tasted like rubber in my mouth. I hated to admit it, but dinner with Rusty would probably be much tastier.

Pam peeked into my room and asked, "Is everything okay?"

"Not now, Pam."

"Text the man the address," she said as she closed the door.

Plopping backward onto the bed, I put the plate on the nightstand. *Why am I so stubborn?*

CHAPTER NINE

KAYLA

No Scandal Tonight

"I'll get it!" Pam yelled when the doorbell rang an hour later.

I was in the kitchen washing dishes.

"Who is it?" she asked through the intercom.

Rusty's voice was on the other end of the intercom, so I made haste exiting the kitchen and heading to the front door. I'd texted him back and told him we should plan to go out another night. Obviously, he ignored me. "Don't let him in, Pam," I whispered. "Tell him I'm asleep."

Instead of being my accomplice in getting rid of him, Pam hit the button to allow him entry into the building. "Ooops," she said, looking at me with wide eyes and a smirk on her lips.

"Thanks a lot, Pam!"

She raised her hands as if she were innocent, then stepped aside.

I flung open the door and examined Rusty, hand folded midair. I gave him a once over from head to toe. When my eyes landed on his handsome face again, I wasn't nearly as upset about him popping up as I pretended to be. "I didn't text my address, so how did you find me?" I asked.

"I found it saved under the wrong name. Can't rely on devices for everything, you know? And that's coming from me, a man who makes his money in tech." Rusty extended a big bunch of flowers to me. "Here, these are for you."

The flowers were a beautiful gesture, but I didn't expect to see him tonight. I was still caught off guard. "I sent you a message asking for a raincheck," I said as the scent of the fresh flowers wafted to my nose and made me smile.

"I received your message," he said. "I still came over because I want to show you there is no reason to be nervous about hanging with me. It's only dinner."

"I'm not prepared to go out tonight. It takes me a while to get dressed."

"I'll wait for you."

Pam reached for the two dozen red roses. "I'll take these, Kayla." She then turned to Rusty and added, "Kayla and I were just talking about you."

The scowl on my face made her pause. "Thank you for taking the flowers, Pam," I said with a look that begged to be left alone, so I could handle Rusty on my own.

"Yeah, so I'll go find a vase to put these in." Pam mouthed, *"You will thank me later,"* and winked before she walked into the kitchen.

After pushing him outside, I noticed he wore a Givenchy tee and fitted slacks. His face looked freshly shaven with a beard that fit his firm jaw to perfection. My body immediately responded to the hunk of a man standing in front of me. "Showing up like this wasn't a good idea. As you can see, I'm not dressed for a date, and it would take me too long to get dressed, so we have to do this some other time."

He nodded. "I knew you would say that, so I bought you this."

Rusty's driver, who stood inconspicuously on the corner wall, handed three bags to him. Rusty placed the bags in my hands.

"If the ones in the bag don't fit, I have different sizes in the car."

Curiosity wouldn't let me hand the bags back to him. I peeked inside the first one. It contained the Rolan Mouret diamond-cut fit and flare black dress I'd been admiring when we first met. A size medium and would certainly fit. A pair of Gucci ladder strap heels was in the second bag. The third bag held a Gucci clutch.

This was well over five thousand dollars worth of clothing. I knew because I'd been saving up to get this ensemble. The clutch was over a thousand dollars alone. An internal war transpired over whether I should take these gifts. My mind kept telling me to at least take the clutch, but I said, "No! I can't—I can't take this from you. It's too much," I said, though I absolutely salivated over the contents of the bags.

"You have no choice but to take them, Kayla. They are yours, and if you don't take them, I'm just going to leave what's in the bag and all of the other sizes at your door," he stated matter-of-factly.

"Rusty, we barely know each other. I can't accept—"

"Are you special?" he asked.

"What kind of question is that?"

"I believe you are special and deserve more than these gifts. Trust me, there is more where this came from." He touched the side of my face as a heartwarming smile turned up the corners of his cheeks. "You said, for our first dinner date, you wanted me to treat you special. This is the start of your special treatment. So take the bags, go inside and get dressed. Allow me to give you the things that will help make this the night of your life." He held the bag out to me once again.

The night of my life, or a night of Shondaland on TV? The choice wasn't very difficult. "Our second date is the same day as our first. Shouldn't we go out tomorrow or something?" I pressed. "You know just to space our dates out?"

Rusty leaned close enough that I felt his heated breath next to my ear. "I can't wait for tomorrow. Get dressed and give me a chance to show you that you'll enjoy yourself with me tonight."

Reluctantly, I took the bag and looked in at the contents again. The diamond-cut dress wrapped around my curves beautifully when I'd tried it on. The heels and velvet bag were gorgeous accessories for the dress. What girl wouldn't love to wear a slinky outfit like this while on Rusty's arm?

My eyes met his hopeful ones and the deal was sealed. I was going on a date. "Alright, I'll go. But I still need time to get dressed."

Worry lines slowly faded from his forehead and he smiled, displaying beautiful, white teeth. "I'll wait as long as it takes."

"Are you sure? I didn't know you were coming and it takes me a long time to get dressed," I warned.

"Go. I'll wait on you... as long as it takes," he repeated.

I walked back into the apartment ahead of Rusty, bags in hand.

Pam wore a sneaky grin on her face when she said, "I can see why she likes you so much. You're persistent about what you want. My type of guy."

My jaw tightened, and my eyes narrowed into slits. She had been eavesdropping from the other side of the door.

"Don't get mad at me, Kayla," she whispered. "He might be a keeper."

I narrowly agreed to this date, and Pam was already calling him a keeper. Well, maybe?

"I am a persistent man. Time will tell if I'm a keeper," Rusty told Pam.

He heard her...ugh!

He whispered close to my ear, "So you like me, huh?"

His hot breath sent a shiver down my spine and that shiver moved all over me. His nearness shouldn't be affecting me this way. My face burned with embarrassment. "Rusty, if you don't mind having a seat, I'm going to get dressed. I'll be out as soon as I'm done. Come with me, Pam." I grabbed her arm and dragged her to my bedroom before she reported to Rusty everything I told her about him.

An hour later, I quickly pulled Flexi rods from my hair as I glanced at the clock. It felt as if I were fighting with the devil to get ready. While time seemed to slow down before our coffee date, it appeared to fly by with each minute tonight. "Pam, will you help me with this dress?"

"Sure." She stood from the bed and walked over to me. As she was zipping the dress, she said, "You left the tag on. Let me get that." She grabbed a pair of scissors, flipped the tag over, and gasped.

"What? Is the zipper broken?"

"It better not be. This damn dress is...Did you see these price tags?"

"Yes, I know how much everything costs. I've been eying this dress for months. I had all of this on my wish list, the shoes, dress, and purse. Rusty saw me window shopping for it when we first met." My heart fluttered as I thought about the thoughtfulness that went into him getting these things for me. He remembered each piece and he picked the correct sizes.

"Rusty sounds more and more like a keeper. How many men remember the clothing you're checking out when they bump into you?" Pam asked.

"None I have dealt with. I can tell you that."

"Right, but he's rich and knows how to impress, so you still have to be careful. Keep the juice box on lock. A few gifts don't entitle him to even one taste," she asserted and adjusted my dress.

"I can manage my box, ma'am. Now, put this on, please." I held out a diamond necklace to her, which matched the diamond earrings I wore.

She gushed with pride when I spun around and looked at her. "You look so good, Kayla. That man is going to eat you up."

"Maybe he will, maybe he won't," I said teasingly.

"Don't get a spanking."

"If I'm lucky, I will."

"You're bluffing."

I laughed.

Glancing at the full-length mirror, I felt incredible in the black dress and strapped heels. Finally satisfied with my look, I grabbed my clutch filled with foundation compact, lip gloss, and ID.

"You are gorgeous!" Pam said, hugging me.

"Thanks, Pam." I hugged her back. "I would still be getting dressed if it wasn't for you."

Rusty rose to his feet when I walked into the living room. His eyes roamed over my body, head to toe. "Holy fuck...you look breathtaking, Kayla," he said with wide-eyed surprise.

Smiling, I looped my arm in his outstretched one. "Thanks. You have good taste in clothing. I hope I didn't take too long getting dressed."

"No, of course not. It was worth every damn minute," Rusty said, leading me to the door. "And you're the one who has great taste. I was just following your lead." He gestured with his hand for me to walk ahead of him out of the door.

Pam spoke up, "Have a great time, you two. Don't do anything I wouldn't do." Then, she came to the door and watched me off like a mother watching her daughter leave for prom.

"You have to excuse her. She's a bit overprotective," I said when we reached the limo. "And again, I'm sorry I took so long and about my place. I didn't know you were coming. I would have cleaned up for you."

Drinking me in like an alcoholic with a fifth of whiskey after a month's drought, he dismissed my worries. "Pam is fine, your place is nice, and you look too good to apologize for how long it took you to get undressed."

I quirked a brow at him.

Rusty then seemed to realize what he'd just said. "Uh, I meant— get dressed."

I laughed.

The limo driver opened the door to let me in.

"You're already undressing me, and we haven't pulled out of the parking lot? Good thing I like you, as Pam said." I winked at him.

He smoothly slid into the seat beside me. "I knew you liked me." His gorgeous smile surfaced. "And, forgive me for putting my foot in my mouth."

"I find it positively endearing, especially after you were so persistent about tonight's date. A little fluke only makes things more interesting."

"About that—" he began.

"Let's just enjoy the night." I looked out the window of the limousine and watched cars pass by as I wondered where he was taking me.

We pulled up to the most expensive restaurant in the city. I'd heard it was so expensive that the prices weren't on the menu. Never in my life, even with my modest savings, would I be able to afford a casual meal or for the tab to be a surprise at the end. I had to budget my money and think things through ahead of time. "This is a nice place," I said, looking around at everything which seemed to be made of crystal.

Which fork would I even use at this place? Would I remember to place my napkin in the right place? Damn, where were the etiquette rules when I needed them? I couldn't remember a thing from Mrs. Santone's eleventh-grade etiquette class.

Oblivious to my worries, Rusty took my hand and guided me toward the front door. Upon entering the large, sliding double doors, we were escorted to a private room. He'd reserved this room on a few hours' notice and I couldn't help but wonder who the restaurant had to kick out to accommodate us.

I slid into the seat he pulled out. He sat across from me as I opened the menu and gasped. "They have cheeseburgers?"

"Yes. Their burgers are delicious."

I didn't expect this place to have burgers. "Wow, I thought they would only have steaks and lobsters."

"They have those too."

"Cool. So, how much is the burger?" According to the menu, the burger had a black truffle, gold leaf, and a bunch of other trimmings I'd never tasted. There wasn't a price listed for it.

Waving my question away, Rusty continued to scan his menu. "Don't worry about the price. Just order what you like."

"I was just curious. You said you ordered it before."

He put down his menu, and his eyes met mine. "I didn't really pay attention to the price, but I think it was a couple grand for the burger."

My eyes grew wide. "You spent a couple grand to eat here?"

"No, that's only for the burger. I usually have the home fries, wine, and salad, which could add another grand to it easily."

Dizzy. That's how I felt. A couple grand was a paycheck for me. *What am I doing sitting here with a guy who could eat my paycheck for lunch? What can we possibly have in common?*

Rusty reached across the table and took my hand in his. "Kayla, I'm successful. Very. Successful. And I don't apologize for it. I worked hard to get here, so please don't judge me because of it. I eat here because the food is good and I can't take the money with me when I die, so I enjoy it now. Are you okay with eating here?"

Nodding, I said, "Yes." I had financially profiled him. Just because he had buckets of money didn't mean he thought he was better than me or that he planned to use me.

I relaxed by the time the waiter walked over to our table to take our order.

After a quick greeting and run down of the house specials, he asked, "What would you like to drink tonight, sir?"

"We'll have a bottle of Dom Perignon and give me the shrimp scampi," Rusty said.

"Um... I'll have the lobster." If a burger was in the thousands, I dare think about how much the lobster was. I would have to work years to pay for one meal.

Sitting back in the chair, I took a drink of my hundred dollar a sip champagne. The numbing effects of the alcohol calmed me, so I relaxed even more.

By the time dinner arrived, Rusty and I were deep in a conversation.

"So, there Pam and I were, alone in Vegas, behind bars and drunk off our asses, then she turns to me and says, 'Okay, I can get us out of this, but I'll need some whip cream, a nail and a box of condoms.'"

Rusty's shoulders shook with laughter as I told him old stories about Pam and me.

The waiter tried unsuccessfully to maintain a professional expression as he listened. He sat our meals in front of us.

I stared down at my plate curiously.

"Something wrong?" asked Rusty.

I expected a hearty open lobster, so I could enjoy its insides without having to fight with it. On further reflection, I was glad that wasn't what showed up. I got a perfect cube of lobster meat with some sort of yellow sauce drizzled across the plate. It did look beautiful, but would the flavor live up to the razzle-dazzle of the looks? "I just didn't expect it to look so good," I admitted. "Damn. Now, I feel bad that I'm messing it up by eating it."

The waiter choked back a laugh. "Enjoy your meal." He gave a small bow and vanished from the room.

I took a bite and moaned in pleasure. It tasted absolutely delicious. The most delightful bite of anything I'd ever tasted. The yellow sauce was some sort of lemon butter.

I had to give it to him. The man knew how to treat a lady. As for the restaurant with the thousand dollar burgers, they were on point with the food.

"Thanks for such a lovely evening," I'd said, once we were back in the limo.

Rusty wrapped his arm around my shoulders. "It's only the beginning."

I felt happy to hear this because I didn't want the night to end.

We looked out at the many people who were out enjoying the crisp, cool night. I snuggled up close to Rusty, warm and sated. He held me snug to him as I inhaled his woodsy essence into my being. I logged every detail of him into my memory.

The driver drove around the city, eventually stopping at Promontory Point. Rusty and I got out then walked over to get a good view of Lake Michigan. Enraptured by the calming waters under the surrounding night lights, I slipped out of my heels and walked barefoot on the smooth rocks.

Rusty caught up to me and pulled me into his embrace. "Would you like to go back to my place for a nightcap?" he whispered the words against my earlobe.

The feel of his lips against my flesh rendered me speechless. Being here with him under the moonlight with the majestic beauty of Chicago's skyline and the reflection of a castle-like structure behind him, I was willingly under his spell.

Going back to his home while feeling like this would only lead me to one place—his bed. I'd be rendered powerless once in his domain. My desire for him was too strong. Pam's admonishments struggled to make their way to the surface of my mind, but the feel of standing under the moonlight in his arms won.

My breathy answer flowed freely on a sigh, "A nightcap would be lovely."

CHAPTER TEN

RUSTY

Not That L-Word Again

We barely made it into the elevator before I had Kayla pinned against the wall, drinking from her plump lips. I was thirsty for her. She desired me too, gauging by the way she pulled me into her, clawing at my shirt, ripping buttons as she tore it open to run eager fingers across my chest. I wasn't particularly gentle with her clothing, either. She was disheveled. Her stockings were ripped in the center by the time we exited the elevator. I grabbed her hand and pulled her in the direction of my apartment.

"Your home is lovely," she said as she stepped over the threshold and into my domain. Her eyes alighted upon the living room design.

"Thanks."

"I love the floor to ceiling windows," she continued to compliment my home.

She was stalling. Maybe I was moving too fast. "I chose this design so the space would feel bigger," I said, taking deep breaths to control my breathing.

She bit her bottom lip as she narrowed her eyes at me. "You did a good job."

I cupped her chin and kissed her, slowly suckling at her lips. I captured her tongue for a mating ritual so natural that I felt a piece of my self-control slipping away. "We don't have to do anything you don't want to do," I whispered against her lips.

"What if I want to do more? What then?" she asked.

I lifted her off her feet. Her legs wrapped around my waist, and I palmed the globes of her butt with my hands. Upon entering my bedroom, I eased her to the floor, backed her to the bed, and pushed her onto it. Her dress hiked up at the bottom while hanging down below her breasts at the top. I licked my lips as I breathed in her sexual aroma. "Your scent has been driving me crazy all night. I have to taste you."

"Mmmm," Kayla moaned with the first swipe of my tongue on her wet silky folds. She wanted more, and I planned to give it to her.

"You're a hungry little minx, aren't you?"

"Your hungry minx," she teased, placing her hand on my head to press me closer to her mound.

As she ground her hot pussy into my face, I ran my hands up and down her soft thighs then brought her closer to me. I dove my tongue into her sticky tunnel of love and twirled it in her sweet juices. I could see myself becoming addicted to her delicious flavor.

"It feels so good! Oh—" she moaned.

My cock throbbed with intensity as I pleased her. I doubled my efforts in bringing her to ecstasy, licking her with quick, targeted strokes. "Come for me," I demanded as my tongue darted in and out of her slit. It all happened so fast and I couldn't believe I was pleasuring her while enjoying every second of it. I wouldn't exchange her flavor for anything at the moment.

"Rusty," she cried out, her voice thick with passion.

"Kayla." The sound of her name on my lips turned me on unlike ever before. "Darling Kayla," I had to repeat it.

"Ohhh, I'm coming!" Her thighs tightened around my face, gripping me for dear life. "Oh, my goodness, I'm coming so hard!"

I pried her legs apart and thrust my tongue into her heat like it was my cock. I had no intention of letting her go until her plentiful orgasm gushed into my mouth. I greedily swallowed all of her sweet juices down my throat once that orgasmic moment was realized. I finally stood after I gave her nether lips one more lingering kiss, groaning as I did so. She watched me hungrily as I tore open a condom and rolled it on. I couldn't get inside her fast enough. She was dripping wet when I thrust into her. And fuck me, she felt so good.

Fuck. Fuck. Fuck.

I didn't know how long I could last inside her hot sweetness that clung to my cock like a sheathed sword. I grabbed her hips and angled her upwards. This wouldn't be slow, sensual lovemaking. Just a frenzy of desire. Two mad beasts, rutting. Waves shot through me with each of my pounding thrusts.

*I...She...We...*felt perfect as one.

She curled her hands around my sheets, balling them up in her fists.

It was so fucking sexy watching her squirm under the pressure of my rock hard cock. I leaned down and kissed her breasts, sucking her budding, brown nipples between my lips.

She whimpered, her fingers now laced in my dark strands. Wrapping her arms around my neck, she held on tight.

I slipped my hand down between us and rubbed her slit as I stroked her long and hard.

"I'm coming, again— Fuck..." She stared into my eyes, ferociously, as if it pained her to receive so much pleasure.

Her dirty words mixed with the intense look in her eyes made me increase my already relentless pace. My release was coming as well, and I yearned for every drop of it. "Come for me, Kayla," I muttered against her upper lips as I massaged her swollen lower lips. "Cover me with your sweet cum."

Time seemed to stop as she peered into my eyes. Her carnal gaze spoke to me and ushered the cum right out of my balls. I barely had control of my own body from the moment I connected with hers. I twitched inside her and came hard at her pussy's insistence. A guttural groan roared from deep within my throat, then I collapsed on top of her, drained. "Kayla. You are amazing."

"You are too, Rusty."

We were in a tangled mess of sweat covered clothes. As the night wore on, we ditched the clothes and cuddled naked underneath the covers. Several times throughout the night, we woke each other and made love.

Love. There was that word again.

I slept holding Kayla in my arms like I never wanted to know life without the warmth of her body against mine. I had a night without dreams. There was no need to dream when a woman like Kayla Johnson laid by my side, her sweet essence intermixed with mine.

CHAPTER ELEVEN

KAYLA

Stay With Me

So this is Rusty von Strauss' idea of a nightcap, I thought when the first light of morning hit my face. Recollection of the most fantastic night flooded my mind. I lie there wrapped in his arms in his huge circular bed, watching him sleep. The man looked even more handsome while sleeping than he did when he was awake.

Being in his penthouse the morning after such a beautiful night seemed surreal. The impromptu date, the gifts, the dinner, and our intimate tango had all been fairylike. Rusty was a wonderful man who kept me laughing and talking all evening while we were in the restaurant. Then, when we made it back to his place, I'd been most pleasurably ransacked until we finally drifted to sleep, too exhausted to ravage one another anymore.

But what we shared probably screwed everything up. Going home with him so soon couldn't be a good thing. This had been our first real date, after all, and I had been an easy lay. Damn, I hated to admit Pam was right.

"Morning, beautiful." He awoke with a smile in his eyes. He placed a small peck on my lips and then reared his head back to study me. "What's that look for?" His penetrating stare was a reminder of the love we'd made. How did he know my body through and through?

I rested my head on the pillow and looked at the ceiling. "I can't believe we did that last night."

"Which part?" he asked with a tempting smirk on his lips. "The date? Sitting under the moonlight at the lake? The nightcap? What part can't you believe?"

"Well, I went home with you on the second date. Did coffee even count as a first date? Did I sleep with a man after one date?" I spat a stream of questions and huffed.

"I'm not going to let you do that." Rusty put his arms around me and rolled me on my side, so I faced him once again. "You didn't sleep with 'a man,' you slept with me, a man who's into you."

"You're into me, huh?" I asked with a teasing smirk.

"Yes, I am, Kayla. By some standards, this..." He pointed his finger to himself and then me. "...is considered premature, but I set my own standards in life. I like you, so don't question this...us. I know how to differentiate between genuine and fake. What happened last night was as real as it gets." His eyes were intense as he stared at me.

My heart fluttered under the pressure of his glare. I'd never get enough of the way he looked at me. I leaned in and kissed him firmly on the lips, so hard that our breaths became fluid gushes of air depending on one another for suction and release of oxygen.

"You feel that?" he asked as our kiss ended.

"I feel it, Rusty."

"There's something very real between us."

"That's what scares me. Things are moving so fast, and I think I'm falling for you from the top of your head down to your silken ivory toes," I said and giggled. I don't know why, but the corny words just came out.

Rusty's eyes glazed over with an unreadable expression. His forehead furrowed. Then all of a sudden, he turned away from me and got up out of bed. He stood in the middle of his bedroom with his back to me, just gazing ahead unseeingly.

"Are you okay?" I asked, confused by his sudden change in demeanor.

"Do you want breakfast?" he asked in a muffled tone. His voice sounded as if he were choking back emotions.

"Yes, I would like that," I said, getting out of bed to walk over to him. I missed his nearness. I wanted to wrap my arms around his waist and kiss the muscles on his back.

As soon as I touched him, he jumped. "I'll go start breakfast now." He walked out of the room before I was able to wrap my arms around his waist. He purposely avoided me and I didn't know what I'd said to make the great wall of Rusty rise so quickly.

"Okay, I'll just freshen up," I called after him. He didn't respond, so I went into his bathroom, gargled with mouthwash, and washed my face. I ran my fingers through my hair, which thankfully was still curled, though ruffled. I entered the kitchen wearing Rusty's button-down shirt he'd worn last night.

Leaning with his back against the counter with his arms folded and his hand on his chin, Rusty seemed to be in deep thought and definitely bothered by something.

"Are you okay? You can tell me if I did something you didn't like," I insisted, fully aware the magic we shared last night had faded away within the last twenty minutes.

"I'm fine," he uttered, his tone flat.

Now, I felt like I totally sucked in bed, and he wanted me out of his house. I felt out of place but decided not to be rude. I'd eat breakfast then leave, so I could get dressed for work.

Rusty smacked his hands down on his pants, which snapped him out of his somber trance. He then went to the stove to sauté hash browns and green peppers. He poured some of his creation on a small plate and took a fruit bowl out of the fridge.

"Do you want me to pour drinks?" I asked, feeling the need to help in some way.

"No, I'll get everything. I just want you to relax and enjoy your breakfast."

We ate in awkward silence.

When I finished eating, I took my plate to the sink and rinsed it along with my glass. "That was delicious. Thank you. Everything was lovely," I said.

Rusty nodded but didn't reply.

"Well, I'm going to go get dressed and let myself out," I told him.

"Don't," he finally spoke. Standing, he walked over to me. "Don't leave me." A vulnerable look entered his eyes as he stared down at me.

His intense glare gave me pause. I had a few minutes to spare before I needed to leave for work, so I asked, "Rusty, is something bothering you? Do you want to talk about it?"

"Call in, and stay with me," he said in a direct tone.

"I can't. I have to work."

He took me by the hand. "You can't or you won't?"

"What kind of question is that? I have to go to—"

"Stay with me, Kayla."

I didn't know what was happening with him. One minute, he was eating me up, and the next minute he acted cold and distant. Now, he wanted me to stay. I felt it best to remove myself from the situation to give me time to think about all that transpired over the past twenty-four hours. "I really want to stay, but I have to go. Let's meet back up for lunch later today," I compromised.

"Can you make an exception for me and work from here today?" he asked.

I laughed. "Rusty, I can't just up and work from home. My business is based in the office."

"Are you sure you can't make an exception for little ole' me?" he asked with his bottom lip protruding in a faux pout.

"What am I going to do with you?" I asked, wanting to suck that lip into my hungry mouth. After last night, I would always be hungry to taste and feel his mouth against my flesh.

"Oh, I know what I want you to do with me," he said in his sexy, seductive voice.

"Really? What's that?" I asked.

"Make love to me. Make me forget anyone before you," he said, dipping down to suck my lip into his mouth.

I wanted to revel in the feel of his lips against mine, to accept him devouring me as if I were his last meal, but I leaned away from him and acknowledged, "Whoa, that's more power than I have."

He pulled me by the hand toward the stairs. "I believe you underestimate your power."

I followed with little resistance. When we reached the bottom step, he sat down and pulled me on top of him. I was immediately confined by his arms slinking around my back. I thought he would try to ravish me right there on the stairs. Instead, he just held me close for the longest time. Neither of us saying a word.

"No one has ever been able to make me forget about my pain like you have, especially after one night," he admitted after he stood and allowed me to gently slide to my feet. He turned and walked up the stairs.

Somehow, I knew a reply wasn't necessary. Quietly, I accepted his unspoken invitation and walked behind him to his bedroom. He sat on the edge of the bed and pulled me down beside him. Once I was seated, he stood in front of me, pushed me back onto the bed, and kneeled in front of me.

"What are you...Rusty..." My question faded away as he spread my legs wide and high into the air, resting them on his shoulders. He drowned out my trepidation of the unknown by inserting his tongue into my canal. His licks to the underside of my throbbing clit caused me to raise my hips off the bed. His hands cupped my breasts, his thumbs and forefingers stroking my erect nipples in unison.

His tongue went deeper inside, up and down, until I screamed out and cursed his name. He then glided his tongue to my naval, where he playfully inserted it there. He continued to slide slowly up along my stomach, stopping below and in the center of my chest. Placing his hands on the sides of my breasts, he squeezed them together and gave both of my nipples a soft kiss. He put both of my nipples into his mouth and began to suck. "I don't want to let you go," he blew the hot words against my sensitive skin.

I squirmed beneath him, thrusting my dripping wetness toward his hard steel. I reached down with my right hand and grabbed his cock. It was throbbing in my hand. It couldn't get any harder, I was sure of it. I guided him to my slickness. I wanted him so bad, more than I ever craved what's his face. I couldn't even think of his name. Not in this moment of heated desire. Just as Rusty had wanted me to do for him, he'd made me forget everything before him. The head of his cock entered me and took control of my every fiber. My greedy entrance swallowed him hungrily, accepting him as my heated mate.

He thrust his hips faster, penetrating the very depths of me. I drove my hips into his strokes in an attempt to absorb him entirely into me. We were doing the tango of love. He placed his hands on my ass and lifted me a foot into the air. His cock penetrating unfathomable depths, deeper than I'd ever been touched. He plunged and plunged, fucking me fast and ferocious.

"Ohhhh!" I screamed out as the bed rocked beneath us. The lamp on the bedside table shook, but he still continued to fuck me without any care for our surroundings. It seemed like he was trying to stamp out something deep within the both of us. His hardened length reached down into my soul and yanked—a powerful, groundbreaking climax from me.

He rolled over onto his back and pulled my trembling body on top of his. I quickly got into position to ride his strokes. Jolting when he entered me again, another vibration of ecstasy shot through me. My pussy lips squeezed his cock each time he entered me. I reached down with my left hand and squeezed his balls.

"You're a naughty girl, Kayla."

"Do you like it when I'm naughty?" I asked.

"Hell, yes, you feel so fucking good. You are excellent, Kayla. Fucking excellent!" He placed his hands on my shoulders and pressed down with each thrust. Now, he was penetrating me so very deep, filling my inner walls until it felt like a volcano was about to erupt from inside me. The rumblings of that eruption could be seen in the dirty way I looked at him—lip biting, squinted eyes, wrinkle lines on my forehead.

Rusty continued his sweet assault, and I surrendered to it wholly. The sweat from his brow dripped upon my breasts and nipples, making them glisten. I closed my eyes and drifted to another galaxy. I couldn't take it anymore. My body began to quiver uncontrollably. I held onto Rusty for dear life as he held me high in the air. He thrust into my hot slit four more times, deep. After the fourth thrust, he stayed connected with me, gently rocking as he gave both of my nipples another soft kiss. He placed a tender kiss on the right side of my neck and whispered into my ear, "Thank you, thank you for giving yourself to me. Now, fuck me, baby, like I've never been fucked before."

His kinky talk drove me to a new level of wildness. I began bucking above him, and soon, a gush of cum squirted out of my slit onto his stomach.

At the sight of me squirting, Rusty came hard while whispering my name in my ear, once again telling me how he didn't want me to leave. "Stay with me today."

"Baby, I have meetings set up already," I said. As much as I wanted to stay, I had other people depending on me for their companies' success.

"Call off."

"I wish it was that simple."

"Darling, it really is that simple. Do you want me to do it for you? Who's your boss over there, Helen?"

"Rusty, you can't be serious right now," I said, pushing away from him and lying on the soft, white blanket. Even if I wanted to skip work, which I kind of did want to, I wouldn't have him call in for me. I shot him the side-eye before gently pushing him in the arm. "I handle my own business when it comes to my career."

"Point taken. I guess I am a bit overzealous."

"Ya think?"

We both laughed.

"Besides, I have the boss from hell. I'd be hitting up soup kitchens and the Red Cross for rent assistance if I call out an hour before I'm due in. I have to get out of here and get home to get dressed, by the way. I'll be calling in late as it is."

"Darling, the least of your worries is soup kitchens and rental assistance. You just so happen to have the unwavering attention of someone who will make sure that you have everything you need."

I opened my mouth to speak.

"However..." He cut me off. "I do respect that you have a career that you worked hard to build."

"Good. Okay. I'll see you tonight?" I asked.

"You most definitely will."

I got out of bed and put on my clothes.

Rusty laid back and watched me dress, then walked me to the door. His driver waited out front to take me home. Before we went outside, he planted a lingering kiss that solidified my desire to return later tonight.

When I walked through my apartment door twenty minutes later, Pam had obviously been waiting on me, ready to give me the fifth degree.

I held my hand up and said, "Not one word."

"Umm, hmm, look at you coming through here, walking funny," she said from behind me.

Ignoring her, I went into my bedroom with a smile. Rusty von Strauss's name was tattooed all over my body. I wasn't sure I ever wanted to remove his branding.

CHAPTER TWELVE

RUSTY

Claiming Kayla

I'm falling for you from the top of your curly head to the bottom of your silken ivory toes...

It had been five days since I'd seen Kayla, and what she'd said to me continued to echo in my mind. She came back to my house that night. We spent more time together, but aside from phone calls, we'd been too busy to get together through the week. I had to do something to change that. I needed to see her.

"Cassandra, did the advertising department send up their strategy proposal for next quarter?" I asked when I walked into Digitek precisely at eight.

"They did, as a matter of fact." She nodded. "I just received the package in my email. I'll print it off and bring it in with your morning coffee in ten minutes."

"Make it five. Thanks."

Four minutes later, Cassandra bounced into my office with a stack of papers in one hand and a cup of coffee in the other. She set my coffee down in front of me and gave me the papers. "This is the comprehensive budget and plan, and Judie says that it's a solid plan because it includes all media outlets—" She paused and looked at me before taking a few steps back to study me. "Rusty, you look more vibrant than you have in a while. Did you get the dog?"

"No, no dog," I said.

Being one of my closest confidants, Cassandra knew some things about my personal life, but she didn't know everything. Other than my business life, people didn't know much about me, and I wanted to keep it that way.

"If it's not a dog, I must say, whatever you did after you left here five days ago, you should do a lot more of it. You have been chipper. I can still see the smile in your eyes."

If only she knew what put this smile in my eyes, as she put it. "Thanks, I'll take that as a compliment."

"It surely is, boss." She smiled. "Call me if you need anything," she tossed over her shoulder as she exited.

If my day went as planned, I wouldn't need to bother Cassandra for anything. My plan was to familiarize myself with these figures and then head over to Naustram's. But before I did that, I walked into my adjoining bathroom and looked in the mirror.

My eyes are not smiling, are they?

A little while later, I arrived at Naustram and took the elevator up to the third floor. When I was a startup, my Naustram rep introduced me to television, radio, billboard, magazine—all things media. Oh, I remember the good ole days. Only having a few thousand dollars for advertisements and trying to make the most out of it. This place had surely changed from those days. It had grown into a dominant force in media marketing. Every company headed somewhere big had a representative for their brand in this building.

Helen Becket must've been alerted that money was on the premises. As soon as I stepped off the elevator onto the third floor, she approached me. "Russ, there must be a good reason for you to make a personal visit to Naustram today. How may I help you?"

"It's Rusty," I said halfheartedly as I scanned the area, looking for any sign of Kayla. There was no way, shape, or form Helen could help me with what I needed. I wasn't in the mood to have a long talk with her about marketing and ads. I had one mission and one mission only. Taking Kayla home with me.

"I know your name." She giggled. "I'm sorry, Rusty. Is everything going well with your advertisements? Is there something I can help you with?"

"The current ones are going swell. The reason I'm here today is to personally talk about the launch of the Slayed Pages platform. I understand that Jane Heard will represent me in that endeavor."

"That's correct, sir. She's the best!" she replied. "With you being our most valued customer, we assigned our highest producer to your account and will continue to do so." Pride beamed off of her as she went on to talk about how Jane knew the ins and out of media, in every form.

All of this may have been true, but she didn't know the ins and outs of Rusty von Strauss, and at this point, that was all that mattered.

"Let me direct you to her office, so Jane can tell you more about her plan for the launch," Helen was saying as she turned toward a corner office.

"That won't be necessary."

Helen turned back toward me and stared at me blankly before confusion set in her eyes. "Ooookay," she said slowly.

"Effective immediately, I want my rep changed to Kayla Johnson."

"Effective immediately?" she repeated.

Apparently, I wasn't the only one with a habit of parroting.

"Excuse me? Did you just say Ka-Kayla Johnson?" Helen deflated, and her shoulders slumped a bit.

"Yes, Kayla Johnson. I want her representing all of my accounts. I understand that she's a brilliant up and coming marketing expert, and I want her. That won't present a problem, will it?" I asked.

"Why no, I mean yes, Kayla is over our African American business to business accounts, so your account is not in her specialty. Plus, Jane is already doing such an excellent job on your campaigns. It would be very inconvenient to start over with a new person."

"I'll tell you what. Whatever Jane has prepared, I will use it. However, going forward, as in this very moment forward, I want Kayla to represent all of my brands for our media promotions. That part is non-negotiable."

She stood there, speechless.

Since she didn't respond, I continued, "Now that we have that settled, I'll also need for Kayla to spend the rest of the day with me discussing the specifics of how our relationship will unfold, so any meetings that she has set up needs to be rescheduled. My account will be big enough to keep her busy for a long while." My stern tone brooked no room for discussion. Kayla was leaving this blasted place with me, and she would be getting back in my bed as soon as humanly possible.

"Sir, I'm not sure Kayla is ready to run such a big account," Helen reasoned.

"That's my final thought on it. It's Kayla or nothing."

"Yes, sir." Helen finally relented.

"Very good. Point me in the direction of her office."

"It's right over there in the corner."

Before she could finish, I walked away. Entering a decent-sized office, I found Kayla sitting at her desk with a pair of glasses on her face. I didn't even know she wore glasses. She looked hot in them too.

She was writing something down in a notebook while talking on the phone. "That's right, Mr. Hammonds. We want those spots to run during prime time. Yeah. Okay. That's very good. Yeah, during the Kevin Hart special will be great. I'm writing all of this down as provisions of our agreement. They need to be in the contract, as well."

She did this thing where her mouth dropped open and she stuck that pen inside, making me eternally jealous of the glossy plastic and the ink that ran through it. I didn't disturb her. I just wanted to watch her in her element.

"No, it looks like I have everything I need," she said after removing the pen from her mouth and dropping it down onto her desk. She raised one of her hands in the air and brought it back down with a fist pump. Whoever was on the other end of that call had made her day, and I was jealous that he had the opportunity.

"Okay, talk to you soon, Mr. Hammonds." She hung up the phone and said, "Yes!" That was when she looked up and saw me. "Oh, hey!"

"Hey." I stood there, admiring her quietly for fear that words would mess up this moment.

"Rusty, what are you doing here?" she asked, confirming that concern.

"I came to check on my media account."

"Oh, really?" She tightened her jaws, giving me a suspicious glance. The suction motion from her mouth caused my cock to jump in my pants. "Jane's office is a few doors down," she said, bringing my attention back to the lie I was telling about checking on my account.

"I know where her office is," I said and closed her office door behind me. Noticing a vacant desk beside hers, I realized she shared this office with someone else. I would have to change this. My woman needed her own damn office. How else could I come up here and share private moments with her?

"Oh," she stared at me innocently.

"I'll handle my account in a little while. Right now, I need for you to come and greet me like we spent the other night absorbing each other's bodies until the sun came up."

"I can't. I'm at work," she said, looking around. She stood up and walked over to me, stopping just in front of me. She had a giddy look in her eyes, but both of her hands were clenched together in front of her as if she were afraid to touch me in her workplace.

"Come here." I pulled her to me and kissed her, first swiping my tongue across her lips and then jabbing it into her mouth. Soon, our tango ensued and what an exquisite dance it was. Her feline essence escaped her throat in a carnal moan that shot straight to my groin, and my manhood sprang to life with the vigor of a swordsman ready for battle.

Her office door flung open, and Kayla leaped away from me. I reached for her, eager to pull her back into our supernatural force. How she'd broken it was unknown to me.

She shook her head as I reached for her, her eyes growing big as saucers.

I followed them to a plainly dressed woman who came walking in with two cups of coffee.

"You said you were tired, so I brought you a cup of coffee," the woman said, sitting the coffee down on Kayla's desk. "Should I come back later?" she asked.

"Yes, you should come back later," I answered, adjusting my pants, so my erection wasn't on full display.

"No, Sandra, you're fine. This is your office too. Besides, Mr. von Strauss was just leaving. He has a meeting with Jane about his account." Kayla walked back around her desk and was about to take a seat.

I stated, "She's not my rep anymore. You are."

The perplexed look on both Kayla and Sandra's faces was priceless. I wished I had a camera to show the levels of shock, bafflement, and excitement in Kayla's eyes. That right there was the reason I'd made her my new rep. I wanted to bring that out of her. Her face glowed with joy as my news sank in.

"Rusty, what are you saying? Digitek has always been Jane's client."

"Not anymore."

Shock registered on her beautiful oval face, "You didn't?"

"I did and without hesitation. The first thing I need for you to do as my new representative is to have lunch with me."

Kayla's gaze went to Sandra.

Sandra quickly sat down at her desk and busied herself.

Kayla stood there like she was contemplating what to do next.

I took her hand. "We have a lot to discuss about my account, so let's go ahead and get started catching you up now."

"My two o'clock meeting was postponed until we finalize the contract details, so I guess I could devote the rest of the day to learning your account needs," she said with a slight smile.

"See there. Perfect timing, perfect everything," I said, squeezing her hand.

She reluctantly picked up her purse and walked out of the office by my side. Sandra just stared with her mouth agape as I ushered Kayla urgently away from Naustram with high anticipation of the things I would do to her once I got her alone.

"As much as I appreciate landing your account, you can't just come and get me off of my job like this. You're going to have to set an appointment like all of my other clients," she announced once we were in the parking lot. Her earlier perplexity had changed into irritation.

"But I wanted to see you again."

"How about a phone call to set up a date? You didn't have to stroll up onto my job and buy my time. I have a job to do—a job that I do well, by the way."

I touched her cheek and ran my fingers over her soft skin. "And now, your job is to work on my account."

"But this is so messed up." Her words didn't match the sneer crinkling the corners of her lips. "I bet Jane and Helen are seething."

"Let them seethe. I will give you as much business as you need to be the top salesperson at your job."

She touched my hands, gently pulling them from her face. "I want to get there fair and square. I must become the top salesperson based on merit, not based on who I'm dating."

"Listen, it's not my fault you work at a place I do business with. I've only known you for a short time, but after what we shared, there's no way I'm going to do business with a place and not let you benefit from it. Now, if something happens and you become my crazy ex, I'll have to cross that bridge when we get there," I said, in hopes that it would lighten her mood. I wanted her to relax and accept spending the day with me. "Until then, you're going to let me help you get to the top of the sales team."

She smiled. "Okay, let's start with you taking me on a tour of Digitek. Then, we can have an actual meeting in your boardroom to discuss your account," she dashed all the dirty ideas I had of the way we would spend the morning.

"Okay, if a tour and meeting are what you want, a tour and meeting are what you will get," I said and opened the door for her to enter the car.

As she got close to the door, I lifted her off her feet for a hug. Placing her back on her feet, I held her close and used my weight to pin her back against the frame of my car.

Her sparkling brown eyes revealed something. She was tough, but it had to be a cover for the fear she harbored within.

Peering into the windows of her soul made me want to do more than have sex with her, more than work with her. I wanted to know her, far beyond my bed. I wanted to grow with her— this new feeling would be something I needed to get used to.

CHAPTER THIRTEEN

KAYLA

Getting to Know You

"So, Pam calls me at work and tells me, "girl, he's up in his room playing games. I told you his sorry ass wasn't gonna go to work.""

"You sound just like her." Rusty laughed.

"That's my bestie, so I know her through and through," I said, joining his laughter. "But I was on my last straw when she called me. I went to Helen's office and had a mini face-off with her before storming off my job to go home. When I got home, I found him there, just like Pam said."

"What was he doing?" Rusty asked as he offered me a bite of sautéed scallop. I allowed him to feed me, and he held the fork in place for a second to make sure the food made it into my mouth. He wiped the corners of my mouth with a napkin.

I ate the delicious bite and smiled at him before continuing my story about Ju, "He was indeed laying up there in my bed like a big ole thirteen-year-old playing that damn game."

"Oh my..." Rusty busted out into laughter again.

"That's not the funny part. The funny part was that after sitting out of work and laying around like he didn't have a care in the world, he had the nerve to ask me to jump his car battery, so he could crank it to leave *after* I put him out for not working."

Our roar of laughter started together this time.

"Kayla, the way you tell the story makes it seem hilarious."

As I theatrically recounted the story, it was funny. But it wasn't funny when I lived through it. "Thinking back on it, it really was comical. Ju just didn't have any drive for me or himself."

"You know what I have to say about it?" Rusty asked.

"What?" I stuck my fork in the seafood plate we were sharing.

He pushed my hand away, got a shrimp for me, and put it in my mouth.

"Thank you," I mumbled as I covered my mouth with my hand.

Rusty's mood sobered when he said, "I'll never make the mistake of thinking you're not worth working for. I'll get up every day and work hard for you to be happy, whatever that takes."

I put my fork down. "That's easy for you to say, Rusty. Hard work is a part of your DNA. I mean, look at you. You own a successful company that's on the verge of a sale that will put you in the billionaire status. You don't exactly fit in the category with a man whose only means of survival is a temp job."

"Hard work is hard work. It doesn't matter what job you have. Besides, I haven't always been in the position I'm in now," he said defensively.

"You're right. Hard work makes the difference, no matter what your job is. I wouldn't expect anything less from someone like you because you understand what it took to start your tech company."

"Earning money isn't what I'm talking about. What I'm saying is that I'll work to gain your heart, to keep you happy, to keep you safe. I don't want you to want for anything emotionally or physically. Not as long as I'm around," he said confidently.

I leaned my head back against the sofa. "Whoa, this is getting a little too deep, too soon, don't you think?"

Sated with a luminous glow in his dreamy blue eyes, he stared at me and asked, "That depends on your answer to my next question. Tell me what you expect from me. When you think of me, what are your thoughts?"

I cringed at how serious he suddenly became. "Well, for one, I haven't had enough time to form a really strong opinion about you. From what you have shown me so far, I expect you to spoil your women and treat them well. I like what I've seen. I expect you to be passionate about everything that you do."

He raised a finger. "Correction, I don't have women."

I smiled. "Yeah, that's the other vibe I keep getting."

"What's that?" he asked.

"That you have layers to you that you don't want unpeeled. Like you are holding parts of you back, parts unseen." As sure as brightness glowed within his spirit, there was also darkness inside of Rusty. Something deep, possibly traumatic.

"So, you're saying that you'll stick around to find out?" he asked.

I bit down on my lip and looked into his eyes, then willed myself to look away. His orbs were like a captain pulling me out to sea. Stranded somewhere out in the Pacific and unwilling to look for land, I made the mistake of staring out at the beautiful waves of the ocean where Rusty was king. "I couldn't leave if I wanted to. I'm stuck on you," I admitted.

"When you say you're stuck, do you mean that in a good way?" he asked.

"Oh, it's good. I never liked being this vulnerable, until now," I said.

Rusty removed the food from between us on the floor and scooted closer to me. He placed one finger underneath my chin and summoned my face to collide with his, not by physical strength but by the mystical powers in his sea-blue eyes. They sent a ship out to my heart's shore, and I boarded. Before I knew anything, his lips were cruising upon mine like a great explorer conquering my world. I went along for the ride, too enraptured by waves of desire to reel myself back in.

Just as our kiss intensified enough that we were breathing each other's breath, he pulled away and just stared at me. A smile tempted to rise to the corners of his lips. He rubbed his finger over my mouth, assessing the spot he'd just kissed. "You're so beautiful, Kayla."

"Thanks," I gasped.

His fiery gaze ignited my flames. A kiss ensued. A soft murmur passed through my lips as a coarse groan roared from deep in the back of Rusty's throat.

"I can't keep my hands off of you," he said in a raspy tone.

"Why do you even try?" I asked, slipping my hand underneath his shirt to allow my fingers to dance across his chest.

"I just wanted to give you a break from so much sex. The other night we went at it nonstop. I don't want you to think that's all I want when, in fact, I just want to be with you. If it were left up to me, we'd unite as one and only separate for eating, using the bathroom and showering."

I left his embrace and stood. I walked over to his mantle and put my hand on the side of it. "We have spent a lot of time connected this past week, haven't we?"

"Not nearly enough."

"I've never had anyone like you, Rusty."

"What do you mean by that?"

"I mean, you came to my job and just snatched Jane's account right out from under her," I said with a snicker.

"Is that a bad thing?"

"Heavens no."

Rusty let out a sigh. "Good, because it was partially a selfish move, but I do want you to have my business."

"See, that's more than all of my past boyfriends combined have done for me."

"I'm obliged to be the first to treat you like you deserve to be treated then." He walked over to me, took my hand from the mantle, and pulled me into another of his heated embraces.

"It's too early for me to feel the way I feel, though."

Rusty's eyes darkened when he leaned back from our hug and searched mine.

I felt the urge to understand what he was searching for. I wondered if he actually knew how quickly and hard I was slipping under his spell. "I'm falling for you, Rusty. Please don't let me fall if you have no intention of catching me," I uttered before his head bent, and our lips met in a mind-numbing kiss. His tongue claimed mine warranting every swipe by being so damn delicious. I would forever remember the feel and taste of this man's lips and tongue against mine, long after he stopped being so damn mystical. These types of moments always came to an end in every relationship, didn't they?

He groaned as his lips left mine and searched hungrily for my chin, neck, any area of skin not covered by my dress. He forced a thigh between my legs, urging them apart. The firmness of his leg settled between my thighs and nestled against my panties, encasing my swollen, pulsating flesh. The throbbing only dissipated when he slipped his hand inside my panties and stroked my slit with adept sensuousness—not too fast, not too slow.

119

Throbbing became the least of my worries when Rusty stuck his finger inside, and finger fucked me. His quickening pace caused my breath to catch. I thought I had been breathless before, but at this very moment, I fought for my life to breathe. My pelvis rocked to grind against his finger while I desperately grasped for something to hold my balance...anything. "I'm about to fall," I gasped.

"I got you. Forget it all and just feel Kayla. Feel this. Feel us."

He didn't understand. I was literally about to fall onto the floor. "You can't hold me. I'm going to fall," I murmured, trying to get control of my legs and the orgasm threatening to ravage my body.

"I'll catch you." Rusty groaned into my mouth. "Let go and feel everything, every bit of this."

I swallowed his words into my being as he repeatedly jabbed at my sweet spot. I trusted him because I needed to. When I let go, the most explosive orgasm shot through me, causing my knees to buckle. Catching my balance was the least of my worries. "Uhh, Rusty," I crooned out.

"Does that feel good to you, baby?" he groaned as he ground his thick finger into my heated slit. His free arm supported my weight as he pressed me against the wall.

"Yes!" I cried out. But it was better than good. Try magnificent, wonderful, splendid, delightful—all the good things. My body was sensitive with my back against the wall as he patted my pussy with his hand.

"I promised myself I would spend today getting to know you, but you see what you do to me?" he whispered into my ear, his hot breath blowing steam against my eardrum.

"Oh, so I did this all by myself." I grinned coyly. "Looks like I had a little help." I looked down at his hand, still inside my panties.

"I lose all self-control when I'm around you. You are truly an awe-inspiring woman." He slipped his hand out of my panties and walked back over to the sofa. He sat down and motioned with his hands for me to come and join him. Tugging me down into his lap when I reached him, he lifted his fingers to his nose and inhaled my natural fragrance. "Um, so what do we do now?" he asked.

We shared a laugh. Then, I wiggled out of his lap and sat down on the sofa beside him. "How about this? I told you about my last relationship. Tell me about yours," I suggested.

Rusty's jawline tightened as he stared off into the corner of the room but didn't seem to be looking at any particular thing. "Her name was Meagan, and she broke me," he started. "Well, it wasn't exactly her that broke me. It was the prospect of what our love was supposed to fix that did it. Circumstances with the woman before her actually left me a broken man. It was Meagan who put a lock on the tomb that I thought I'd forever buried when it comes to my love for another woman."

"Wow, that sounds pretty severe. What did Meagan do?" I asked, knowing it must be a doozy of a story if it had him this visibly upset. I leaned into the sofa and watched as my man— *My man?* Yeah, I internalized it as a thought, even though I never said it aloud– poured his heart out about his past loves.

"I thought Meagan and I were in love, but she stole from my bank account. She was a gold digger."

"Oh, how sad. It's terrible when people steal from you. So many people don't want to make their own money these days." I thought about Ju. Though he'd never stolen anything from me, I felt like I could relate to Rusty being taken by his ex.

"To make matters worse, she gave a good chunk of my money to her father as an investment for one of his businesses, which has become my competition. Have you heard of Mighty Pages?" he asked.

"Yeah, I think Sandra does some media for them."

"She probably does. They're kind of well known as of late because of a windfall they received for advertisements. The money used to start that business was taken directly from my bank account by his daughter, Meagan."

Shocked, all I could say was, "You're kidding me! That's pretty messed up."

"So you see, you're not the only one with a story about someone who drained you dry," he admitted.

"You're right about that."

"Unfortunately."

"You mentioned a love before her. Who was she?" I questioned.

Then, he did it again—looked off into the corner of the room, at nothingness. When Rusty finally turned back to me and looked into my eyes, he was miles away. His voice sounded faint and solemn when he said, "Kayla, I'm getting tired. I think we should call it a night. I'll have Wendell drive you back home now."

"So you're putting me out, just like that? I thought we were having a good conversation." This was the second time he went cold on me. The first time, I didn't understand what happened. This time, it was because of the mention of the woman he'd loved before Meagan.

He yawned loudly and excessively, stretching his arms into the air. "I have a meeting with more investors tomorrow, so I'm going to turn in early."

I gently pushed his shoulder. "That's a cop-out, and you know it."

"No, it's not. I do have to get up early," he said defensively.

"I don't doubt that you have to get up early, and I don't doubt that you have early morning meetings, but when I asked you about the other woman in your life, you suddenly were ready to end the conversation. That's the mystery about you...this other woman, whoever she is."

"I don't want to talk about it," he said, and the sudden change in his demeanor was troubling, to say the least.

"Ooookay. I'll leave then." I stood to leave. "I guess I will need that ride from Wendell unless you want me to call a cab." I took one step away from the couch toward my shoes.

He pulled me back down beside him. "Don't be upset with me," he said just above a whisper near my ear.

"What's going on with you? One minute you're hot, and the next, you're cold. Tell me what's bothering you." I searched his features for any sign of the truth. Why did my bringing up this woman from his past rattle him so? Who was she, and why did he act so distraught over her?

"It's nothing you should worry about, Kayla."

"Okay, I won't worry about it anymore." I wrestled myself free of his grasp, picked up my shoes, and called a cab. "Just let Wendell have the evening off. My cab will be here in twenty minutes."

"Cancel it. I won't have you riding home in a cab this late in the evening. Wendell won't have a problem taking you," he said, sounding defeated but persistent about my safety.

I stood by the front door and crossed my arms over my chest. "Fine, I'll wait for him."

The twenty-minute wait it took for Wendell to arrive to "fetch" me was the most awkward minutes of my life. I'd been completely open and honest with him about every part of my life, but something haunted Rusty, something he wasn't ready to open up and discuss. This was no way to begin a relationship.

CHAPTER FOURTEEN

RUSTY

Complete Me

It took a lot to talk Kayla down off the ledge of leaving me last night. I told her I would call Wendell to pick her up, but I had no intention of letting her walk away from me, especially not with the thought in her mind that I didn't want to open up to her. I just needed time and I would tell her everything.

So, as she stubbornly waited for a ride home, I was able to convince her to spend the night. Now, she was lying across my body, filling me with her warmth.

I spoke softly against her ear, "Kayla, darling, it's morning."

"Oh, man, is it morning already?" she asked, pouting as she spoke. She sighed and then moaned aloud. "I'm tired, Rusty. I don't feel like moving from this spot." She stirred atop of me before falling limp again. "Correction. I can't move. I can't feel my legs."

I definitely knew how she felt. I didn't want to disconnect from her either. She felt amazing. A long night of making love to her made me forget about my troubles and bury my past deep within me. I felt better than I had in quite some time, waking up next to Kayla. Her being here was reminiscent of a much better time, some of the best moments of my life.

My ivory legs intermingled with her ebony ones. A perfect hint of the sun bounced along her skin, making it glow to a beautiful shade of mocha—a sight I logged into my memory for times when I wasn't with her. Watching her was something I could get addicted to.

"Babe, we have to get going," I stated reluctantly. I glanced over at my grandfather clock in the corner of the bedroom, and naughty thoughts entered my mind. "Well, we do have a little extra time before we have to be at work. I can help you work out the kinks in your legs, and you can stay in this bed all day. Helen knows you'll be spending a lot of time with me over the next few weeks, so you don't have to go in today if you don't want to."

"No, Rusty, no. I don't think I'd survive another of your workouts." Kayla giggled through a blush and tried to shimmy away from me. "Besides, I have other clients than you," she said feistily.

I flipped her over and pulled her beneath me. I kissed the side of her face, inhaling her in as I did. A deep groan escaped my throat as I took in her essence. It was no longer her own. It had become an apogee of us.

Kayla was right. If I started making love to her, it would be well after eight before either of us made it to the shower—if we even made it out of this warm, comfortable bed. "You're safe this time, and this time only, Kayla Johnson."

She sighed and a flush rushed to her cheeks.

This woman was too sexy for her own good. I could just eat her up. I crooked my neck and sucked her lips into my mouth. Her lips parted and I eagerly sought out her tongue, tugging at it to absorb as much of her as I could before I released her. "So how many ad spots do I need to buy so that you outsell Jane Heard?" I asked as her fragrant, warm body disconnected from mine.

"About three hundred thousand would put me in a clear lead. But I don't want you to buy them all. I want to earn the top sales record," she reminded me.

"Baby, you have earned every dime of what I'm going to spend," I said with a weak laugh, totally spent from making love to Kayla throughout the night. I'd successfully talked her into staying with me after finding a way to make her feel comfortable without having to talk about Paula. Now, work was calling us both by our full names, and we had to answer the call.

I'd told Cassandra to hold any calls that weren't dire. Surprisingly, she didn't call and interrupt my day yesterday. This was a new day, though. I had a meeting with two investors who couldn't be ignored. Digitek Inc. quite possibly would be in a higher tax bracket within a matter of a few hours. I had to get up out of bed and head to the office, despite how badly I wanted to settle into Kayla's groove and become one with her once more. Kayla likely was eager to get back to work after spending the day with me, as well.

"Rusty, I want to work for it," she repeated as she smiled.

"Okay." I rolled away from her in the bed and took a deep breath. My burgeoning steel was rock solid. "Since we're pressed for time, you should find a change of clothing in my guestroom. Once you are dressed, Wendell will give you a ride to work."

"I'd prefer to go home and get dressed, Rusty."

The intense look she shot in my direction gave me pause. "What was that look for?"

Her scowl intensified. "So, you just keep women's clothing in your home for the random tramps who visit?" she asked.

"Yes, I do," I answered in a measured tone. The implications of my offer resonated with me as soon as she replied. "The first part of what you said, but not the latter. None of the women I bring here are tramps."

"So, you bring a lot of women here?"

"Kayla, why are you getting so upset? It's just some things I keep in there for my aunt when she visits." A flat out lie. I knew it and from the look on her face, she knew it too.

"Yeah, right. Funny, you didn't mention *any* living relatives when I told you all about my parents and everyone else that's close to me. Now, you have an aunt that drops by and doesn't bring her own clothes." Her head tilted to the side while she looked at me as if picking a guy out of a line up who'd just stolen her purse.

"Are you saying that you don't believe me?" I asked.

128

"The way I see it, you have a guestroom with women's clothes in the closet. The same way you are offering for me to put them on, you could be offering them to other women, that's all. I'm not trying to argue. I'm just stating my opinion."

"You're the only person I've ever offered to wear the clothes in that room," I said defensively. This part was true. There had never been a woman to come here that I felt was special enough to go in that room, much less ramble through the closet and have her pick of the clothes in there. Meagan probably could have gotten away with it, but she was too busy shopping for her own clothes to even be concerned with the things in Paula's closet.

"I wasn't born yesterday Rusty." Her voice rose a few decibels. "And I know you didn't just start fucking when you met me. There's no need for us to lie to each other about anything, so if you have other women who come here, just say it now. You don't have to play games with me. I can handle that shit."

"I can't believe you're saying such foul things."

She huffed. "Foul things like what? We've been cursing at each other all week, just when we're having sex. Don't act like you're Mr. Goodie now." Kayla got out of bed and went into the adjourning bedroom.

I could hear the hangers screeching against the pole they were hanging on. She walked back into the room with a navy blue two-piece pantsuit. "Your thotties have good taste, by the way," she said flippantly.

"Thotties?" I didn't know what the word meant, but it felt like a dagger straight to my heart. "Kayla, don't fix your lips to say that, ever again."

"Yeah, whatever," she sniped, stalking into the restroom and closing the door behind her.

I followed her into the bathroom. "No, it's not whatever. I need you to understand that you have to be more respectful."

"You know what? I'm sorry. I'm getting way ahead of myself. What are we on like part two of our fuck fest? It doesn't matter whose clothes they are. You're a single man, you can do what you want. Who am I to question you? It's just an eye-opener for me. That's all. Besides, I should be thanking you for another outfit, right?" Her words were harsh, but she looked hurt.

I wanted this to stop. "If you don't stop this right now, Kayla..."

"What? Are you going to put me out? I'll leave!" She stormed by me.

I grabbed her arm, stopping her in her tracks. I pulled her close to me, and she struggled to get out of my grip. "No, I'm not letting you go. Not until you listen to me. I don't know why you're jumping to so many conclusions."

When she stopped fighting, she stood stiff as a board. Then, she sniffled.

Oh shit, she's crying.

"The only thing different about you and Ju is your skin color and your lie is different. He lied and said he was going to work, and you're pretending that you don't entertain women here all the time. I'm not special to you, so stop trying to boost me up and have me falling for you like this." She waved her arms around, gesturing toward the bed we spent the night in the night prior.

"That's below the belt. I'm not pretending with you," I retorted.

"Everything with us is below the belt," she said, hurt filling her voice. She looked at me, disappointed that I had women's clothes in my house or because I'd been secretive about it, I wasn't sure which one.

"You mean more to me than that, Kayla. Sure, I can't say that I'm ready to marry you right now, but I definitely want to explore this and see where we end up."

"I never asked you to marry me. I just want you to be honest."

"Okay, the clothes belong to a family member. That's the truth."

"Your aunt?"

"Just trust me that it's completely innocent."

She searched my eyes for believability for a few seconds. Then, her features softened. "Fine, I'll wear the pantsuit."

"You can have that suit. I know it's going to look good on you," I said, and thoughts of the owner of that suit flashed through my mind causing pain to engulf me once more. This time, I didn't succumb to it. I remained strong for Kayla. She was my 'here-and-now.' "As a matter of fact, anything in there that you want is yours."

"Are you sure your quote-unquote aunt won't care?" she asked, narrowing her eyes to slits.

My, my, my, she is a handful. "I'm positive that you can have anything in there you want. Wear the suit; it will be perfect for you."

She raised her shoulders and held the blue suit up to her body, sizing it up. Something flashed behind her eyes. This something told me she believed the wardrobe in Paula's closet was completely innocent.

Watching as she admired the piece of clothing, I knew it would look regal on her. Paula wore it well, also. My heart lurched at the thought of her no longer being here in this big house and no longer being able to enjoy her possessions. "I'm going to grab a shower in the guest bath. You can shower in here," I offered up my roomier master bath for her comfort. I wanted to afford her every convenience I could give her.

"Thanks, Rusty. Are you sure you don't want to join me?" she asked.

My voice shook as I answered, "We better not do that since I have that meeting." Memories from my past surged from deep within me and resurfaced.

"Okay, Rusty. I'll surely be lonely in here," her voice faded into the distance as I walked away... feeling incomplete.

CHAPTER FIFTEEN

KAYLA

Don't Make Me Angry
You Won't Like Me When I'm Angry

"Good morning, Miss Kayla," Sandra said when I walked in and sat at my desk.

"What?" I asked, suspicious of the way she was grinning and ogling me with her head tilted slightly. I wore the regal suit Rusty gave me, and it meshed to my body, fitting every curve to perfection. In fact—too perfect.

"Everything is clear now. Chicago's richest tech geek strolls through the door, asks for you by name, and changes you to his account's rep. Then, I walk into our office and find him doing his best to extract your tonsils from your throat with his tongue being the extractor. Honey, do you know you snagged a billionaire?"

I giggled. "Ummm...can I plead the fifth?"

"No way."

We both laughed.

"And you know Helen's head is spinning, right?" she asked.

"Why? Did you tell her about the kiss?" I asked.

"No, honey, but she talked my ear off about him coming up here and changing you to his accounts. She tried to find out what I knew about you and Rusty, wanted to know how he knew you, and a laundry list of other questions I had no answer for."

Sandra's questioning gaze let me know she wanted answers as well—answers I wasn't prepared to give her at the moment. "That's typical Helen. She's not going to rest until she knows every detail. I really wish Rusty wouldn't have come up here and done that. It's only going to cause more problems between Helen and me."

"Uh, huh. You're right." Sandra eyed the pantsuit I wore. She got up from her desk and walked over to me. "That's an expensive-looking suit you're wearing. Is it Armani?"

"Yes, it's Armani. I do splurge on myself sometimes," I said, which was true, even though this wasn't an instance of my splurging. I didn't usually buy Armani suits for work. When I spent more than a few hundred dollars on one item, it would be for a cocktail dress or something I wore during my leisure time. I only hoped my poker face was on. I had no intention of telling anyone in this office about the extent of my relationship with Rusty.

Sandra wiggled her brows. "Yeah, and I'm sure Mr. Rusty had a little something to do with your recent splurge."

My office phone rang, giving me a much-needed escape from Sandra's questioning. I had been about to tell her I had a lot of work to do, anyway, so I gladly used the phone call as a diversion. "It's a beautiful day at Naustram's, Kayla speaking. How may I assist you?"

Sounding disheartened, the caller said, "Hi, Kayla, Mr. Nullent here. I'm disappointed to hear that you will no longer be working on my account. I really liked working with you and would've preferred to have kept it that way, but I understand that you have a larger account that you've been assigned to and that you will no longer have time to work on mine."

"Is this what Helen told you?" I asked as my eyes traveled to the cabinet with my client's files. I stood up, peeked in, and realized all of the Nullent documents I'd prepared were missing. "This is my first time hearing this," I informed him.

"Yes, she called me with the news earlier, and I just wanted to let you know that you will be sorely missed," Mr. Nullent said.

I could hear the concern in his voice over whether his account would be adequately handled going forward. "I'll have to speak with Helen to get some clarity on this, but rest assured that all of the reps here are qualified to take your business to the next level," I remained a team player. I didn't want to let Mr. Nullet know just how livid I was to have been removed from his account after all the work I'd put into growing it. "And as always, if you have any issues, you can call me, and I will be glad to help you." I wanted to keep the door open in case we ended up working together again in the future.

"Aw, now that makes me feel much better," he said with a sigh. "Good luck with your new client."

"Thank you, Mr. Nullent. Goodbye."

Just as I hung up, Helen strolled through the door as if she knew Mr. Nullet would call me after getting the news of my dismissal from his account. Her eyeglasses sat on her nose as her beady eyes peered over them at me. "Did you and Mr. von Strauss go over his account yesterday?" she asked as her greeting. This Rusty business seemed to be eating her alive. And she would whatever was in her power to get back at me.

"I'll get to that in a minute, but first, did you take me off the Nullent account?" I asked.

"Oh, yes, that account now belongs to Jane, seeing as how you will have your hands full with Digitek." She walked further into the room and over to my desk. "I've been trying to understand what Mr. von Strauss could possibly see in you that would make him kick Jane off the account and put you on." Helen glared at me like I was a piece of gum on the bottom of her orthopedic shoes. "I keep coming up with nothing."

"Why don't you ask him?" I retorted. "Or better yet, do you want me to call him up, so you can ask him that question just the way you presented it to me?"

"Call him if you want," Helen countered. "But it seems as if you don't value the blessing you have in working here. Your attitude sucks, and you need to adjust it."

I stood up from my desk. "My attitude sucks?" I adjusted the collar on my suit and walked around to her.

"What sucks is you taking an account from me that I worked hard to get and that I'd all but closed the deal on. Now, Jane gets to say that sale is hers when Mr. Nullet would have never come to Naustram had it not been for me."

"Oh, don't give yourself credit where it isn't due," she snapped. "The work done on that was so sloppy that Jane is going back over everything and reworking it."

I knew this was a lie because I followed our procedures to the letter. She was only trying to get underneath my skin. "Let me tell you one thing. From this day forward, you will show me respect, or I'm going out the door, and I'm taking Rusty's business and any of his associate's business with me. Do you understand what I'm saying?" I asked.

"I never had anyone speak to me like that! Kayla, you are out of line!"

"Nah, you have never had anyone speak to you like that because you have never met anyone like me. What you're about to do is get in too deep, messing with me."

She gasped and put her hand over her heart, then glanced in Sandra's direction.

Sandra burrowed her head into her desk and pretended to be engrossed in the papers sitting on it, her way of saying she didn't have anything to do with our debate.

"You can't talk to me like that. And threatening to take Naustram's clients can land you in a lawsuit that you will never recover from," Helen warned.

I walked to my desk and sat down while Helen stood there with her mouth agape. "I'm not concerned about being sued if you're not concerned about stealing my commissions and giving them to Jane. You see, just because a person is cordial with you and tries not to come out of their nature to match your nastiness doesn't mean they are a pushover. Make this your last time addressing me inappropriately, Helen. Um-kay?"

When she didn't respond, I asked, "Is there anything else I can help you with? If not, you can excuse yourself. I have a lot of work to do."

I stared at Helen until she turned on her block heels and stormed out of my office, slamming the door behind her. If it weren't for Rusty's influence at Naustram, she would have happily called security to have me escorted out the door.

CHAPTER SIXTEEN

RUSTY

Keep Pulling Me Back

I left my office after a grueling meeting with two investors and drove to Kayla's apartment. I needed her to take me out of the misery of spending the last twelve hours without her. Work had required my time, spilling into the evening hours. Now that my magnate duties were done, she was my priority. So, I dialed her number and waited patiently.

"Hello," her melodic voice answered on the third ring.

"Kayla, why has Wendell informed me that you weren't at work when he came to pick you up?"

"Because I have my own car, and I wanted to come home and get in my own shower and get dressed in my own clothes if that's okay."

"It is, but the plan was for you to be picked up. Are you also going to make an excuse not to come over tonight?" I hoped not.

"I'm not going to make any excuses about anything. I really just wanted to come home and didn't think to call you," she stated calmly.

139

"Well, you could have worn some of my cousin's clothes from the guestroom," I offered.

"Your cousin?" She paused. "Wait a minute, I thought you said those were your aunt's clothes."

"They are my aunt's clothes. What did I say?"

"You just said they were your cousin's."

"I meant to call her my aunt. She's actually my mother's cousin, but because they were around the same age and were raised together, I was raised thinking she was my aunt," I tried to clean up the mess I'd made by saying the wrong relative.

"Well, is she your cousin or your aunt?"

"I consider her my aunt, but she's actually my cousin. Going forward, I'll just call her my aunt."

"Right," Kayla said slowly.

I imagined the stress lines forming on her forehead as she overthought my slip up. "Now that we have that cleared up, are you going to explain to me why you're being stubborn and not coming back to my place?" I asked.

"I'm just acting like an adult woman who has her own place to stay. I came home because I live here."

"But you're my woman."

"Oh, really? I've decided that the next man I date will have to work hard to earn that title. As of now, you're not my man. I'm not your girl. We're just getting to know each other."

"And doing some amazing things to each other while lying horizontally...do not forget that part."

"I haven't forgotten," she admitted breathily.

"Well, open your door because I'm about to get to know you some more."

When she opened her front door, the first thing I noticed was her eyes, slanted and dark brown, locking with mine instantly. Then came the rest of her gorgeous face, young and beautiful with just the right hint of ripening to keep her from looking pubescent. Stunning. Against my will, my eyes slid down to drink up her sexy body, lean without being skinny and just enough plumpness to stretch out the fitted dress she wore in a way that made me imagine what was underneath.

The appraisal itself couldn't have taken more than a few seconds, but it felt like a lifetime. Thankfully, I wasn't the only one making an inspection. The way her eyes hugged my features told me she missed me too.

"Hey, Kayla."

"Popping up again, huh?" Her gaze lifted. The slightly predatory smile spreading across her face hit me like a punch to the loin. "Come in."

Ignoring the sudden and inexplicable stutter of my heart, I greeted her with a long hug. She smelled heavenly. And, she was soft...sink into slowly soft. "I missed you. That's why I came here to see you."

"But we just saw each other this morning," she said.

Whatever excitement I'd felt dissipated when I glanced at her roommate, who sat on the sofa, scrutinizing our every move. I needed her gone so I could be alone with Kayla. I didn't even have the patience to wait until we made it back to my house. I was sure my constitution wasn't that strong.

Kayla's voice cut through my internal monolog. "Would you like something to drink?"

"No, thank you. I'd rather we go back to my place if you don't mind."

Kayla's brow rose as she realized my intentions. Her smile was no less effective than the first time I saw it. "We can hang out here since you're already here," she suggested.

"Yeah, we could, but—" I stopped myself. What was I supposed to say? *'I want you to go with me because I'm going to fuck you as soon as we hit my front door? I want to hear you scream my name at the top of your lungs and I don't want to have to deal with a nosy roommate?'* She'd probably kick me out for telling her what I was thinking.

"But what?" she asked.

"I have something special waiting for you at my place." If I counted as being something special, this wasn't a lie.

Kayla chuckled. "Follow me back here for a second, so I can grab my things."

We walked back to Kayla's room. As soon as the door closed, she gripped the hem of my shirt and peeled it off. Without another word, Kayla's hands moved to my pants. I watched as she stripped herself down to her silk panties and knelt in front of me. For possibly the first time in my life, I was struck speechless.

Kayla peered up at me, her expression a strange mix of innocent and wicked, clearly waiting for something. "Did

142

you really miss me?" she asked, her bottom lip poking out in a tiny pout as she ran a hand over my smooth chest.

"You're damn right, I missed you." My voice was gruff, almost unrecognizable.

"We have to do something about that then," she whispered. A seductive grin danced across her face. Her eyes met mine, and she leaned forward and nuzzled her cheek against my thigh.

My gut clenched in anticipation. My manhood showed more interest by the second. I blinked as my brain finally caught up with the shock of it all. This sexy, kinky minx kneeling at my feet was mine for the ravishing. My throbbing erection was more than happy with the situation.

Shaking my head in silent pleasure, I forced myself to take a step back, ignoring the discontent I felt at the loss of contact. "Come here."

I guided Kayla to her feet and kissed her with all that I had. I sucked her lips into mine as my heart plummeted. I dared to think I felt the first twinge of true love. The thought alone sent me into a tailspin. Sudden weakness began in my legs. The strength in my arms decreased, and they seemed to dangle at my sides. I was actually moving on, letting go of my past, and I felt defenseless against the movement.

Bemusement crinkled Kayla's features. She cocked her head adorably. "I want you to go to Alabama with me to visit my parents," she said.

This brought my attention back to her eyes that held the same passion taking over me. Without giving it a second thought, I said, "Just tell me when?"

"Monday."

"I'm there."

"Are you sure you're ready?" she asked.

"Ready when you are... Monday," I repeated.

A blush spread across her face as she watched my reaction. The irony would be the fact I was willing to give her anything she wanted before I hit the door. Of course, I'd follow her to Alabama. I'd follow her anywhere. Meeting her parents was a small feat compared to the giant I became when I was with her.

My gaze narrowed as I watched the expressions shift across Kayla's face. She was so fucking irresistible when she blushed. The impressed look she shot me made my cock twitch in remembrance that it was supposed to be buried in her hot, wet pussy by now. I smiled and drew a hand through her thick mane with a sigh. "Listen, I want you to go over there and lay down with your ass up for me. I'm going to fuck you now."

Kayla paused for a moment, considering my order. I could see a glint of defiance in her eyes. Something in this look, something I couldn't quite put my finger on, had me harder than I'd ever been.

Ignoring my request, she gripped my cock with her warm hands and began stroking. She dropped down to her knees and took the head in before my entire cock disappeared into her seething hot mouth. Up and down my shaft, she sucked, slurping and gasping every time she swallowed my entire length. Her pretty brown eyes peered up at me, beseeching the cum from my balls.

I was spellbound. So much so that I did what I never imagined doing to her pretty face: fuck her mouth furiously. Gurgling sounds escaped her throat with each thrust, but she didn't move, didn't flinch, just took every inch of me into her hot throat, ushering the cum down her throat.

Kayla's eyes smiled at me. A tiny huff of laughter hummed against my flesh as I shuttered in the aftermath of my ejaculation. She stood and hurried over to the bed. She positioned herself on her stomach and rubbed her heat from the back.

I could hear the splish-splashing sound of her wetness. Like gravity, I moved to her, my cock lengthening with every step I took. "God, you are going to be the death of me, woman," I muttered, shuddering at the thought of actually plundering her until there was no end.

After a long, rough day, I deserved this moment. With a quick bounce and twist, I took a stroll through heaven. The way Kayla's body enveloped me, bouncing back and connecting with my every stroke, the look on her face as she peered over her shoulder, had me fighting the urge to come within the first ten seconds. I never considered the implications of feeling this powerless. I ran the show with the women I hooked up with. I was the one in control.

"Take me! Get it, Rusty. Own every inch of me!" Kayla screeched out as she drove her backside onto my cock.

The sharp edge of want and *need* in her voice unraveled me again. Orgasmic rapture loomed on the horizon. Hell, I could see it over the clouds. I could feel the joys of it and smell its magnificent air. It had come for me so that I could float away.

"Like that?" I asked, grinding into her as hard as my body could go.

"Oh, Rusty, yes! Fuck me right there. That's my spot. So damn deep!"

"I want to own you, Kayla. Are you going to let me have you?"

"Do it. Just fucking do it. *Own me!*"

"Can I keep you with me?"

"Yes! Yes! You can keep me, Rusty. Keep. Me," she panted.

A thin blade of panic sliced through me as I plunged eager strokes into Kayla's pliable body. "I want you for more than just a night or weekend. I want you forever," I confessed, flicking my finger across her clit vigorously.

"Keep doing that, and I'm yours. Yours!" she boldly stated. The sound of her melodic voice soothed me, giving as good as she received.

I never thought my heart would be ruled by a woman ever again, but at this very moment, I didn't want to ever know what it felt like to not be ruled by Kayla Johnson. "Forever, Kayla?" I verified.

"Yes, forever, Rusty..."

The love we made was second to none. I shook my head, but I could do nothing to shake off the effects of embracing her suppleness. I was ready to give her full access to my world. Her legs pressed against me like an anchor, holding me hostage. With her anchoring me like this, there would be no way out of her love's trap. And I damn sure wasn't trying to get out.

"Oooh. Shit, I feel it coming, Rusty!" she screamed.

"Let it go, baby," I murmured as I slid even closer to her, zeroing in on her slim back. I leaned down to plant soft kisses up and down her spine as I stroked in and out of her hot sheath. "I'm going to come inside you now," I said as my speed increased beyond my control.

"Yes, yes. Give it all to me!" she begged.

Releasing together, we fell down breathlessly onto the bed. The beautiful moment shattered with the peal of my phone. I came back to reality, unwillingly. I sat up and fumbled for my phone, glaring when I saw a text from Cassandra.

Damn the woman and her imperfect timing. I wasn't sure if I felt relieved or pissed off. On the one hand, I'd been waiting on Cassandra's text to give me an update on the software disaster we had at work earlier. On the other, I'd been about to kiss Kayla's lips and make love to her again, roommate be damned. Frustrated, I dragged a hand through my hair, opened the message, and read it.

"Everything okay?" Kayla asked.

I looked into her soft and questioning eyes. And fuck, I had so much to say to her. So much that she wouldn't understand. "It's my assistant. I have to leave," I said, keeping my composure.

"Leave? Are you serious?"

"Yes, it's...important. I told her specifically not to call or text me unless it was important. I just have to go."

"Oh, so, now I'm not as important as that phone call? Let me get this straight, you come over here and command I go home with you. You won't take no for an answer. Then, we have sex, your phone buzzes, and you're out of here. Sounds suspect to me, but go ahead and leave."

"Kayla baby, I don't mean to disrespect you, but I have to go."

"Well, I said go! And don't call me 'baby' when you're disrespecting me by leaving my bed after getting a text," she snapped.

"I have an emergency I need to handle." I didn't have time to argue. The contents of the text spooked me to the core. A true emergency awaited my attention.

"I don't understand you, right now," Kayla stated.

After pulling my blazer back onto my shoulders, I was fully dressed with one hand on her bedroom door. "What don't you understand?" I asked.

"I don't know; one minute you're gung-ho about us spending time together, the next you're running out. I guess a simple text is enough to get you out of here without an explanation. I guess I'm just supposed to settle for the okie-doke, but that's not me."

"There's a problem with the software we created for the new platform. It's fragile with a potential crash lurking. I have to get that corrected before we roll it out to the apps I created. I have to get in the office before the whole thing fails." I lied. I couldn't tell her the truth. Not now. It would break her. Worse, it would break us.

"Well, you should've just said that in the beginning. Why are you always so mysterious?"

"I don't try to be, babe. But look, I have to go." I turned to her and took her by the hand, pulling her behind me to the front door. I didn't want to leave, but my presence was needed at the hospital.

"I'm sorry for grilling you." Kayla smiled up at me. "But I wouldn't do that if you'd just be straightforward with me. I guess I'll have to be more understanding of the demands of your career if we are going to make this work, huh?"

I planted a searing kiss on her lips, which I hoped would help her understand that everything would be fine. My phone buzzed once more in my hand. I looked at it and then back at Kayla. "I'll call you later tonight."

I left out the door, rereading the messages I received from Cassandra.

I need you to call me ASAP.
They called about Paula.
It's time.

A deep-rooted sadness washed over me as I walked out of Kayla's apartment door. Cassandra's text brought the sorrow that had become a part of my core to the surface. Leaning against the railing to recover from the flustered feeling overwhelming me, I took a moment to grieve. It. Was. Time.

Through my mental fog, I made it to the car and hopped in. "Wendell, I need you to get me to the hospital quickly."

I had to go be with the first woman I ever loved as she transitioned—Mrs. Paula von Strauss, my ex-wife.

CHAPTER SEVENTEEN

KAYLA

I've Fallen
And I Can't Get Up

Before I closed the door behind Rusty, he'd turned to me and kissed me like it would be his last opportunity to do so. I'd received that kiss and held onto it for dear life. I leaned against the door, grasping it for the last strand of his energy that lingered in the air.

The sound of Pam's voice brought me back to reality. "Girl, I heard y'all in there tearing it up! I thought I was going to have to call the paramedics for both of you." She giggled.

"I now know for sure that he's going to be the death of me," I admitted as thoughts of the explosive time we had deflated after he received the text.

"That's what he said about you when you were back there, putting it on 'em." Pam stood up and started humping the air simulating what she thought me and Rusty had done in my room. "Shit, with the way you two were going at it, I can't believe you didn't chain him to the bed to prevent him from leaving. It sounds like you were really putting a hurting on each other."

Her description made me chuckle. "Oh, Pam!" I spun around in a circle and wrapped my arms around myself. "I miss him already."

Pam stared at me with wide-eyed bemusement. "Oh, my God! You are *so* gone, Kayla. I should call the shrink now because you're gone."

"Go ahead. I doubt it will help."

We laughed.

"You're making me want to call a tried and true to see what I can get popping," Pam said. "Maybe Greg will come through and tune me up, seeing as how all of this stroking is going on around here."

"Girl, you better leave Greg where he's at, or else you'll never get rid of him. But what did you do, cut the TV off and listen to us? You know what? Never mind. I'm just not about to have this conversation with you."

"Nah, you were that loud." Pam burst out laughing. "I'm pretty sure the neighbors know Rusty's name by now," she sang out in true Trey Songz fashion.

This conversation with Pam was why I didn't like to have sex when she was home. I didn't want to hear her mouth about it. But every moment had been well worth her teasing, up until the instant Rusty had to leave.

"I kinda wish I hadn't given him the goodies. As soon as he got them, he got a text and left in a hurry. I wanted us to spend the evening together, but he had to go handle something at work."

"I'm sure he's very busy," Pam rationalized. "But I know how you feel. No one wants to get screwed that damn good and be left alone." She giggled. "At least you have memories that will hold you over until the next time you see him." Her giggling ceased and was replaced by a serious look.

"What's that look for?"

Pam huffed. "Oh, nothing. Just with all of the lovey-dovey magic being sprinkled around this apartment lately, I'm a little jealous."

I shook my head. "Aw, I don't know one man in America that can handle your feisty butt. And I'm just getting to know Rusty and praying he's not a fantasy in my head like the fantasy I made up about Ju being a good guy that could change."

"Just stay aware. You'll know if he's right," she said thoughtfully. "As far as I go, when my Mr. Right comes along, he's going to be just as fiery as I am, and he's going to know what to do to tame me."

I gave her a high five. "You better know what to say."

"I could tell Rusty didn't want to leave, though. He kissed you like his life depended on that shit. I sat here watching like somebody had turned on a real-life Lifetime movie right in front of my eyes. It was amazing to watch."

My smile broadened. "Oh, Pam, he is too perfect. He quiets my cynical spirit and makes me more optimistic about love. I just don't want to wake up and realize that it isn't real," I divulged.

"Take it one day at a time. Don't think about the end right now. Just be in the moment. The truth will reveal itself. It always does. Trust me." Her words were encouraging. "Didn't Ju's true colors come out?"

"Yeah, and we know how long it took me to snap out of that. Rusty has to be real with me. I hope he won't let me fall too deeply until I can't see a way out. I'm tired of losing in love. This time has to be right."

"I know, but like I said, friend, time will tell."

CHAPTER EIGHTEEN

RUSTY

I Need You

If there is a God above, why does he torment me so? I looked to the heavens and wondered this very thing five years ago. My stomach churned into knots when Wendell pulled up to the hospital. This had been the place where my entire life had changed. The day I got called home from work and found out the man I was would be no more. All of my prospects of having a little Rusty or little girl that looked like my wife were put to rest the day that dump truck collided with Paula's Audi A4.

I'd been hiding my history with Paula from Kayla since I met her. I actually felt bad for not being honest, but how could I just say, oh by the way, 'I was married, but I left my wife because she was terminally ill?' She wouldn't understand that I'd been urged by Paula to sign divorce papers. That was Paula's wish, not mine, and I'd somehow bottled up the sorrow of honoring her wish and kept a tight seal on it.

Paula's wreck changed my life. It made me less of a man. She was the omega to my alpha; where she began, I ended. Paula was the right one for me, my forever goddess...the only woman built from her mold, a mold created just for me. When she pushed me away, I became stuck somewhere in the middle of alpha and omega, wandering aimlessly.

I remember the day I met Paula. She floated around the church, basking in her own little piece of heaven on earth. The moment I laid eyes on her changed everything for me.

"Thank you, Lord, for putting it on my heart to come to this church. You're going to make me a believer yet," I'd said as I looked up to the ceiling at a mural of Jesus hanging on the cross above my head. I talked directly to Him, who'd sacrificed his life just so I could find mine in this church.

I watched her guard the door as an usher. She made sure each person who came through the door had a program and a ray of the sunshine that beamed off her. The service had been interesting that day. The pastor spoke about not allowing anyone to make you feel unqualified. He instilled into the congregation scripture about leadership.

"The Lord will make you the head, not the tail. If you pay attention to the commands of the Lord, your God, that I give you this day and carefully follow them, you will always be at the top, never at the bottom," the pastor said gallantly.

As I listened to readings from Deuteronomy 28:13, I had an epiphany. It was as if God, Himself, had come down and whispered the words into my ear. 'That woman standing at the door...she's your wife. She is meant to be the head and not the tail of your list of prospects.'

I'd been looking for a church to attend since my parents passed away. They were both staunch believers, and they wanted me to be also. When I'd been younger, I rejected being a part of the church, but having lost them both at such a young age, somehow, I felt like I'd be closer to them here.

Needless to say, after service was over that day, I approached her and asked to take her to lunch. "Hi," I said, stopping her from speed walking to the back. "I'm visiting today, and I wouldn't feel right if I didn't take you out to lunch, just to thank you for being so beautiful," I'd said. It sounded like a pickup line, but I spoke from my heart.

"That sounds really nice, but I already have plans with my parents." She smiled brightly. Then, I saw it—the slightest flutter of her eyelids followed by a pink blush rushing to her cheeks.

"Okay, would you like for me to help you with those?" I asked, speaking of the box of programs she carried.

"Sure." She beamed at me. "I've been lugging this box around all morning. It would be nice to have some strong arms help out. I'm taking them to the back office. We could sure use your help around here. You know the church is always looking for new warriors for God's purpose."

"It's my pleasure. Glad to be able to help," I said, allowing her to walk in front of me.

The sight was a delight in itself. A short white skirt rode up her thighs, allowing me full access to toned legs. They had a slight red tint to them, which told me she enjoyed lying in the sun. The cute little white *chiffon top she had on fit close to her waist and fluffed out at the top. Her rusty blond hair had thousands of curls that bounced as she walked.*

Yes, God had indeed revealed my future to me. I was ready to be a warrior for Christ if it meant I would get closer to her. That's what I thought as she turned toward me, and I admired her distinct facial features: a slightly rounded nose like a button, thick brows arched to perfection atop of dark eyes, slick lips lined with golden gloss, and cheeks that looked as soft as cotton. I could tell she wore makeup, but her natural beauty pushed through everything artificial.

"How about I take you out tomorrow?" I returned the topic of our conversation to the date I wanted.

She'd handed over the box to another church attendant by then. "I'll tell you what. If you really want to see me again, meet me back here Tuesday for Bible study."

She reminded me so much of my mother. That sounded just like something she would say. Every answer to my desires was at the church, according to Raynell von Strauss. I loved this girl already, from that moment forward, actually. "Sure, I'll be back Tuesday. What time?"

"We have a sanctified date Tuesday at six p.m." She giggled. "My name is Paula. What's yours?"

"Rusty...Rusty von Strauss. I'll see you soon," I said as I walked off. Well, actually, I backed away from her because I didn't want to lose sight of her until it was absolutely necessary.

We had a long romance that included mostly doing things for the church. She'd saved herself for me and I for her. On our wedding night one year and three months later, I found the other side of paradise when we consecrated our love.

Everything went perfectly until she had the accident. I had taken what was left of my parent's life insurance policies and started up a small tech business, and we'd purchased our first home. We were well on our way to having our happily ever after. But then again, no one was ever prepared for the worst.

Her car flipped off the interstate and landed on its side when she was sideswiped by that dump truck five years ago. Paula hit her head during that accident and severed her spine. She hadn't been wearing a seatbelt. Her injuries were grave. She ended up a paraplegic as well as half out of her mind. Some cognitive disorders were permanent and would be a part of her life for all of the days she had left. I wanted to bring her home, take care of her, love her, be with her, honor my vow to love, cherish, and appreciate her in sickness and health until death did us part. However, with the last strand of her being, Paula used a pen and paper to write down her thoughts. In that letter, she pleaded for me to let go.

I begrudgingly did what Paula asked of me. I slowly removed myself from her life, even signed divorce papers she made our lawyer draft for her. Seeing me made her physically ill, so I stopped coming to visit two and three times a day at first and minimized it to once. Then, I'd go and just look at her through the windows while standing where she couldn't see me. I still visited once a week and just watched her through the blinds of her hospital bed. I never put her in a nursing home. I wanted her to get the best care, so she was put into a rehab hospital, just to hold out hope that one day she'd be coming back to me whole. I imagined us remarrying. I imagined our love restored fully.

Seeing her wither away to a fraction of the woman she used to be caused my heart to lurch in agony. She used to be vibrant and so alive. Indeed, it was her clothes lining the closet in my home. Things I'd been unwilling to part with. As I was prepared to enter the hospital, having not been up here to check on Paula in a little over three weeks, I cringed at the thought of the doctors all saying that her time was near.

Mentally, Kayla had swept me away. Made me forget my heartache. I'd essentially done what Paula asked of me and found someone to love. In this conflicting moment, I felt terrible for loving Kayla. It was supposed to be Paula and me forever. *God, have mercy on her soul.*

I took a step inside the hospital. I hated to see her suffering, but I had to see her before she slipped away from me forever.

"Mr. von Strauss." Lorna, one of the nurses that provided excellent care to Paula, walked up to me when I arrived on the floor.

"How is she?" I asked.

Her dreary eyes told the story of Paula's status. The look in her clouded orbs let me know I didn't want to hear what she had to say. "Not too good. But you can go in and see her. She's sleeping and probably won't be waking up anytime soon since she just got pain medicine."

"It has to be bad. She doesn't like taking pain medicine."

"I know." Lorna nodded. "Look, the doctor will be by to talk to you in just a little while. He'll be able to tell you more about her condition. It's been changing rapidly."

"Okay," I said and walked over to stand by Paula's door.

Before going in, I peeked into the window.

She just laid there, taking shallow breaths. Her jaws were more sunken in than they were the last time I saw her. Her hands and feet inverted and contracted. Her brunette hair thinned out. She looked so helpless.

And so was I, who could afford to buy this hospital, but all of my fortunes couldn't bring her health back. "My love," I said and walked into the room. Approaching the bed, I stared at my wife. Until she left this earth, she would be my wife, divorce or not. The old Paula was in the skeleton lying before me. She remained in there somewhere, in full form, lying there sleeping. "You're going to show these people, Paula. You will make it through this," I told her in a reassuring voice. Hope was all I had.

Paula continued to lie there, still. Measured, shallow breaths visible as the pain medicine effect lulled her into a peaceful sleep.

"Baby, they don't think you're going to make it. Wake up and show them that you will. Make them see what I see when I look at you."

A slight smile curled the corners of her lips. She looked angelic as if she were dancing with the angels already.

I smiled and called out to her again. "Paula?"

She didn't answer. She just kept breathing those shallow breaths.

The monitors attached to her chest buzzed away. I ignored those artificial things, only seeing her. That precious smile and each precious breath she took were the things that held my attention.

"Answer me, Paula..." I called out to her once again, this time hoping a miracle would come into her hospital room and save her from fate.

Dr. Golden swept into the room like a breeze. As a bearer of bad news, he was someone I didn't want to see at the moment. "Mr. von Strauss, this is the day we'd known was coming," he'd said. "Despite our best efforts, the injuries that occurred to her lungs have continued to get worse. Like I told you last time you were here, rehab has been of no consequence to Paula's condition. With her inability to mobilize, she has gone into almost total lung failure. We're at the point where the thoracenteses, the procedure we've been doing to keep fluids off her lungs, are not working."

The doctor spat off medical gibberish, but I wasn't falling for one word of it. At that moment, Paula had a magical glow surrounding her. Her life was not coming to an end. She looked better than she had in years. "Give her the procedures," I ordered.

Dr. Golden looked confused. "Excuse me, Mr. von Strauss?"

"I said, continue to give her those procedures. Keep that fluid off of her lungs. Do all that you have in your power to keep her alive!" I yelled.

"Mr. von Strauss, we have done all that we can do," Dr. Golden said in a pained voice. "I need you to understand."

I grabbed him by his collar and jacked him up in the air. "By God, you'd better not let my fucking wife die! Give her the fucking procedures."

"Mr. von Strass, I know you're upset, but you're lashing out at the wrong person. I'm on your side here," Dr. Golden pleaded.

I dropped him down to his feet, and he quickly exited. He tucked his head between his tail as he did so. "The priest will be in to talk with you shortly," he added before he crossed over the threshold.

My old wounds had been reopened. My soul was bleeding out. No one could see how hurt I was. I sat by Paula's side for hours while tears that desperately needed to fall held steadfast. She wasn't leaving me. She couldn't.

"Mr. von Strauss," a short, slender male priest said when he walked in just as I leaned over and placed a kiss on Paula's tiny, pale hand.

"Shhh, she's resting," I shushed him.

His brow went up and down as he processed what I was saying. "Sorry, sir. Would you like for me to pray for you and your wife?" he asked.

My eyes went from Paula to the priest. I knew she would like to hear his prayer, so I said, "We'd both like that."

"What's your denomination?"

"Catholic."

The priest went into his prayer, "Father, I pray for Mr. and Mrs. von Strauss. I ask that you readily put your hand on Mr. von Strauss, for he is hurting, Lord. I ask You to help them both through this season of transition. A time in which Your sacred branches fall from the tree of life and become one with the earth again. For we know that You gave us life only for the seasons that You allow. I reach out to You, the Father of compassion and the Source of every comfort, asking You to touch Mr. von Strauss with Your unfailing love and kindness. Be the God who comforts him as he goes through this most difficult struggle. They have had a difficult road, Lord, but Mr. von Strauss is holding on for a miracle that only You can provide. Bring them both, Lord, through the tough times ahead. Allow Mr. von Strauss to have purified thoughts that are glorious to Your kingdom, and accept Mrs. von Strauss into Your kingdom when her time grows near, oh Lord. Come alongside Mr. von Strauss in his pain. Strengthen him. May You open his heart so that his troubles and grief may pour out so that he can once again be made whole. Help him find joy, Your joy that will be his newfound strength. Help him to trust You as his God of hope and the God of light. Fill him with joy, peace, and hope by the power of the Holy Spirit. In Jesus' name, Amen."

By the time the priest said his final words, my shirt was drenched with tears. I had slumped down beside Paula, my head resting on her arm. I cried out my last tear for the marriage I thought would be my last.

At thirty-four years old, I would be a widower, divorce decree be damned. As far as I was concerned, I never would have divorced her willingly. A horrible stroke of chance landed me between a rock and a hard place I never thought I would live in.

The priest rubbed my shoulder. "Is there something I can do for you, Rusty?"

I stood up and shook his hand. "No." Short of restoring Paula's body to full health, there was nothing he, or anyone else for that matter, could do. "Thanks for everything, priest."

I wandered out of the hospital room and off the nursing station. My mind numbed by the reality of Paula's impending demise. I had to get out of here at once.

"I'll keep you updated, Rusty," Lorna called after me.

I raised my hand but didn't look back. My heart warred with my rational mind. Did the doctors have it wrong? Was this really the moment when I had to say goodbye?

I'd been in denial long enough. Feeling like as long as I had her in the physical, her spirit was somewhere close by and capable of renewed life.

"I'm sorry, sir," Wendell offered as I somberly slid into the limo. He closed the limo door behind me and ran around to get into the driver's seat.

When Wendell pulled away from the curb, I glanced back up at the hospital, looking at the exact floor where

Paula laid resting. A strong desire to go back in there and breathe my own breath into her lungs to give her life hit me. I would do it. I'd give my own breath so that she can live. Offer me as a sacrifice, instead of her. Surely, there had to be something that could be done.

"Allow me to transcend into the next phase of my life to what is and what will be inevitable, eternal sleep until you awaken me in heaven to let me know you've arrived to join me..." I could hear her voice speaking the words she'd written in her letter to me. I looked around my car. I was alone. Yet, Paula's voice sounded just as clear as ever. She wanted me to let her go, but how?

I gazed to the heavens for the answer. The sky looked unusually bright with many bright stars twinkling above. A crescent moon with radiant edges lit up the darkness. It was a magical night. Were the heavens rejoicing because one of their angels was coming home soon? This thought alone brought me the only bit of joy I'd had since arriving at the hospital. I smiled, even as pain squeezed my heart into its grip and held tight. I rolled down the partition between myself and Wendell.

He looked back into the rearview mirror. "How may I help you, sir?"

"Do you believe in angels on earth?" I asked.

"Why, yes sir, I do," he replied. "I believe that God sends angels in the form of people who are to help us along the way. Sometimes, they are sent to help us get through something. Sometimes just to show us something we couldn't see on our own."

I nodded. "I think you're right, Wendell. Take me to Kayla's."

"Yes, sir," he said and changed the course of our drive.

The sound of the road being soaked up by the limo's tires was soothing as I laid my head back against the leather seat. God might have sent my angel to help me through the most difficult time of my life, but I hadn't realized her true purpose.

"We're here, sir," Wendell said when we pulled up to Kayla's apartment complex minutes later.

"Thank you, Wendell." I took out my cell and called her. I was too deep in thought to think of calling on the drive over. When she answered, I only had the strength to say her name. "Kayla..."

"Rusty, hey. It's late. Is everything okay?"

"I need you."

CHAPTER NINETEEN

KAYLA

Found My Way Back to You

"What is it, honey?" I asked Rusty over the phone, concerned by the morbid tone of his voice.

"I don't want to be alone tonight."

I strained my eyes to look at the clock. It was a little after midnight. "I'll come over now. Just give me a second," I said half-asleep.

"I'm sitting outside your building."

"Huh? You're becoming the king of surprise visits."

"I know. I forgot to call on my way over. I had a lot on my mind."

"Give me a sec to get ready, and I'll be down," I said, once again picking up on the solemnness of his voice. I hung up and sat up in the bed.

Staring into the darkness of my room, I contemplated why I was so eager to jump out of bed and run off on a whim. Just as soon as questions entered my mind, I answered them subconsciously. *You're doing it because you're a woman in love.*

I blew out a breath, stood up, and headed into the bathroom to take a quick shower. By the time I'd showered and was drying off, Rusty rang the buzzer.

Pam entered my room with her baseball bat in hand. "Are you expecting someone?"

"Yes, Rusty's out there."

"What is he doing back tonight? It's after midnight."

"I'm going to find out. Now, step to the side and lower your bat, ma'am." I chuckled at my friend, who was blocking the hallway.

"Oh..." Pam slowly lowered her bat and smiled. "I'll watch you walk down."

I looked back at her as she stood in the doorway, protectively watching me walk to the bottom of the stairway.

Rusty stood at the edge of my steps and hugged me as soon as I reached him.

Pam shook her head when I fell into his embrace. I knew what she thought. This man could call me at the drop of a dime, tell me he needed me and I was there. She was right.

We held one another. He didn't say anything, just held onto me for the longest time. His warmth covered me, along with a gentleness I hadn't felt before.

"Did you miss me?" I asked when he let go.

"Yes, can't you tell?"

"Yeah, well, I missed you too."

We walked to the car holding hands. Rusty helped me in and eased in beside me. My hand rested on the armrest in the middle of the seat, and he placed his atop of mine. My hand shook as he held it. At first, I figured it was because of the chilly night. But the newness of this thing we shared gave me jitters.

He pulled me into his lap and took me into a breathtaking embrace, kissing away my chills and warming me through and through. Once our kiss broke, I moved back over to my seat and sat down. "This feels like a dream," I said.

"My whole life feels like a dream," he said while looking into my eyes. "Some parts I don't want to experience. Others, I don't want to ever wake up from." He claimed my lips once more before he sat in his seat with his heavenly blue eyes trained on the uneventful night.

We rode the rest of the way to his place quietly, him holding onto my hand, each of us looking out of our windows, thinking.

When we made it to his house, he went into the kitchen and poured two glasses of water. "Here," he said, offering me one.

"Do you want to talk about what's bothering you?" I asked after taking a sip and placing my glass down on the marble countertop. He'd been acting differently since he'd showed back up at my house tonight, and I wanted to know why. "Did you get your software issue fixed?" I prodded when he didn't come forth with an answer.

"Everything with the software is fine, but I have something I need to talk to you about," he said with seriousness in his tone.

"You look like death. You're not sick, are you?" I asked.

"No, I'm fine physically," he muttered, slapping both hands against the countertop, then reached for mine. "There is something I have to tell you, and I promise when the time is right, I will. But tonight, I don't want to talk about it."

"You can trust me with any information you have to share, now and anytime," I assured him.

"When the time is appropriate, I will share everything with you. I'm just not mentally ready to tell you what's been bothering me, not after the night I've had," he admitted,

This left me more interested in what he was holding from me. Gently touching his chest, I urged, "There's no time like the present to be open and honest."

His gaze fell pensively on my hands on his chest. He rolled his shoulders as if trying to release tension from his body. Grave anxiety danced behind his eyes.

"I'll wait until you're ready," I relented, knowing right then why I had been shaking in his car. Something was troubling him deeply, and that energy transferred to me. I moved my hands back to my sides and wondered when the other shoe would drop.

"Thank you for understanding, because tonight all I want to do is this..." He took me by the hand and led me into the living room. He helped me out of my jacket and shoes before doing the same for himself. He laid the long way on the sofa, pulling me down on top of him. He drew my head to his shoulder.

171

We stayed like this, saying nothing, just listening to the beat of each other's heart, until my lids were too heavy to hold open and sleep overtook me.

*

Sometime during the middle of the night, he lifted me into his arms and carried me into the guestroom on the first floor. Placing me down onto the bed, he stood and unbuttoned his shirt before sliding down on top of me. He slipped his arm around me. I lay limp underneath the pressure of his lips that came crashing down on mine.

I molded into the plushness of the bed's comforter while being comforted by his hands traveling up to grip the sides of my face. Holding me steady, his sharp tongue clashed with mine. Moving upwards, he seized a patch of my hair into his hand and tugged my head back so that my neck was open for his pillage. His insistent mouth parted. I yielded to his desire to suck my skin, leaving marks of passion wherever he lapped.

The rising tide of desire gushing between us left me dizzy with delight. Wild tremors shot through me, causing me to shake just as I had the night before. Sensations I'd never experienced encompassed my being, taking over and leaving me incapable of being Kayla.

At this moment, I was Rusty's girl. Nothing more. Nothing less. My world as I knew it spun around on its axis once he lifted my long, loose skirt and touched my bare slit. One hand supported his weight as he reached down and unbuckled his pants with the other.

Spreading my legs apart, he thirstily thrust inside of me. Taking no care or preparation other than to toss my leg over his shoulder.

I moaned in pleasure as he ground into my flesh, harder with each unforgiving stroke. Pain and pleasure reeled through me. "Rusty...honey," I screamed.

"You can take it, Kayla."

"I don't know," I said as the weight of his body pushed his thick rod into places unforeseen. It was dauntingly painful and extraordinarily pleasant as I absorbed every inch into me.

"Take it, Kayla. I need you to take it all," he said, rocking his hips to the sound of my forced breathing.

Over and over, he pounded into me, causing pleasure and pain to shoot throughout my body. The exotic smell of his soap, shampoo, and the natural manly scent of all that was Rusty impaled my senses. My mouth watered at the thought of devouring him just for smelling so damn delicious. "I can take it. I'm all yours, Rusty."

He slumped over, and his face felt smooth as it rubbed up against mine. "You feel like silk, so good. I just want to feel this and nothing else," he grunted out.

"Oh. My. God," I cooed. My hands traveled everywhere. Up and down his back. Pushing his ass into my core as I willed his thick, nine inches to plow into me with no remorse.

Anticipating my climax on the horizon, his hand slipped between us to rub intensely against my clit. My legs trembled. My control long gone. A tear fell from my eye as I moaned loudly.

Rusty bucked, stroking me into a stupendous high. His hot seed became one with my womb as I shook beneath him. His lips clung to mine. Hands running up and down my arms. Moving down to my breasts, he latched onto a nipple and sucked greedily. His teeth teased my perky nipple as his tongue slid across the nub.

Sighs turned to whimpers as I raggedly fought to regain strength. I lost that fight when his tongue trailed down along my stomach, dipping inside my navel and swirling around. Downward south he traveled, licking away the residue of cum from my lower lips.

"I found honey," he said, staring up at me.

Those blue eyes caused me to fall back onto the bed to enjoy his warm, velvety tongue slipping in and out of my slit. His torturous movements made me insanely hot. I gasped when his tongue curved inside and touched my hottest spot.

Moans intensified.

Vigorous flickering against my bulb stoked my deepest desires to life.

A small cry escaped me, and the biggest gush of cum poured into his mouth. An out-of-body experience followed as my entire form stiffened, and I fed Rusty the nutrients from my soul.

His tongue lingered around my opening, taking it all in. "You taste just like honey," he said, climbing back up my body. But he didn't take just any ole' hike. He rubbed his way back up, hands reaching my back and cupping my ass in his palms. Slipping back into my depleted body, he made methodical love to me, pleasuring me until we both climaxed again. Falling down against me, he sighed heavily.

Entangled in Rusty's arms, I recalled the amazing ways he'd just ravished me.

"Thank you," he said, sliding his tongue ever so sweetly against mine. Only breaking contact to trail his lips along my neck, shoulder, breasts...

"Why are you thanking me?"

"For spending the night with me. But mostly for making me feel something other than pain again."

"Thanks for returning the favor," I said and sent up a prayer that whatever he had to tell me wouldn't make me regret giving myself to him so freely.

CHAPTER TWENTY

KAYLA

Put Me Together, Again

When I woke the next morning, I dressed in the clothes I'd brought in my overnight bag and went downstairs to the kitchen to prepare breakfast. I paused halfway down the stairwell to just take in the surroundings. His home was breathtaking. I had to pinch myself just to believe I was here. Wall to wall, white on white furnishings: carpet, picture frames, fittings, ornaments. Everything elegantly decorated to fit his great taste.

It took me all of twenty minutes to whip up the eggs, grits and sliced fruit stocked in the fridge. I was pouring two glasses of orange juice when Rusty walked in.

He started preparing his plate without saying anything to me. When he did look at me, he wore a blank expression. The glow of magic we'd shared the night before gone, just like that.

Sick of this back and forth shit... I rolled my eyes as a sinking feeling entered my gut. His mood swings were bearable initially, but the more our relationship wore on, the less tolerant I was of it. What pushed his buttons?

I know he feels this damn electricity flowing between us, I thought angrily as I eased into the chair across from him at the table. "Rusty, you're distant again. What's on your mind? Do you want to talk about last night? When you picked me up, you seemed different."

He looked up, and for a fleeting second, a flicker of cosmic energy passed between us. "No," he replied, causing that moment to dispel. He hurriedly finished his food, flung his jacket around his body, and slid into it. "Thanks for making breakfast, babe."

"Are we leaving already?" I asked, springing to my feet. "I thought we would hang out today and get ready for our trip to Alabama to see my parents."

"About that..." he began. "I won't be able to go Monday. I have to go out of town for at least two or three days. It may be the whole week, so next week is out of the question."

"Oh." I paused. "I didn't know. You said—"

"Yeah, well, I spoke too soon. I have to handle some business that will be final soon." He paused, his tone converting to doom and gloom. The sadness I saw last night entered his eyes, causing them to darken.

"I was looking forward to it. Told my parents and everything," I admitted.

"I promise that as soon as I get back, we're going to Alabama, okay?"

"I guess I have no choice but to accept that since you have something more important to do," I said, offering up a half-smile.

"I'll make it worth the wait," he promised. "I will think of something, sweetness. But for now, I have a lot of work waiting for me at the office. You're welcome to stay here." Rusty's thoughts seemed miles away as he turned to walk toward the door.

The wonderful tunes he played on my body dwindled from the night before. Intertwined in his bedsheets, we were closer than close. This distance didn't exist. Neither of us gave it any room to breathe. It seemed that when we stood vertical, a breeze of coldness kept finding its way in.

Twiddling my thumbs as Rusty got closer to the door, my puzzled mind came to its own conclusions. Perhaps, it was time for our fling to end. Men like him weren't looking to marry the women who came into their lives. Maybe he had the next woman ready to be his miles high lover as he flew to his business trip next week. Sure, he didn't act like the player type, but I didn't have a good track record of discernment when it came to men either.

"Have a good day," I said, having made up my mind I wouldn't be there when he got back. I turned around to walk back into the kitchen. Just as I reached the chair, where I intended to slump down and sulk until I got myself together, a set of strong arms encircled my waist.

Without saying a word, Rusty guided me to turn and face him. He brushed a curly lock of hair away from my face. His dangerously gorgeous eyes peered into mine as he swooped down and captured my lips.

I moaned as his seething kiss reassured me that he was mine and mine alone. With a kiss like this, it had to be real. What kind of man could kiss a woman's lips and have her feel it all the way in her toes and it not be real?

Holding the sides of my face, he owned my lips in the same way that only he could ravish my body. Totally and completely wrecked, I faded away when his hands slipped into the back of my shorts and palmed my ass. "I have to go," he groaned against my ear breaking the emotional moment.

I stood frozen, unable to move, speak, or even breathe. I wasn't even sure if my heart was still beating. When I finally did get my composure, I looked up and Rusty was gone. Standing in his kitchen alone, I remained in an altered level of consciousness. Mind blown. So alive, yet dying because he left me. It's one thing to have sex, but another thing to find a realm of ecstasy with your clothes on.

I gulped in the thick air and turned to my plate on the table. Eating was the furthest thing from my mind, so I tossed the remaining food into the trash and went upstairs to get dressed.

My cell phone buzzed.

Thinking it might be Rusty, I picked it up with a wicked grin. It was a picture message from Ju. It showed him standing in the middle of a factory with a hard hat and glasses on...working. I texted him back.

I'm happy for you.

And I was happy for him. Happy for me. Glad I didn't stick around and try to make a grown man work. Had I done that, I never would've met Rusty, and Ju probably wouldn't have taken responsibility for himself. Everything fell apart and came together perfectly.

"This can't be my life right now. I'm over Ju and in love with a white man," I said, giggling because I never thought I would say those words. Never imagined loving a man without dark melanin. I turned on the shower and stepped in. "And I think he loves me, too." This admission made me smile.

CHAPTER TWENTY-ONE

RUSTY

Don't Want to Lose You

"So, you found the one, but you haven't told her about Paula?" Cassandra asked as we sat in her favorite seafood bar, eating lunch.

Discussing my personal business wasn't my favorite thing to do, but I needed to talk to someone. Cassandra and Wendell were both my employees and my closest friends. "Right, it's like everything has been moving fast." I nodded. "Our relationship has its own wings. It's hard to just stop soaring high with her to talk about it."

"You mean talk about the fact that you're still in love with Paula? That's kind of a big deal, don't you think? You do understand how tabloids work? Suppose the media were to find out you're seriously dating someone. The next thing you know, they'll be digging up your past and writing articles and internet blogs, saying you 'left your ex-wife on her dying bed and moved on with various women, the last of which is Kayla Johnson.' Have you thought about what a write-up like that will do to Kayla? You're not just some average guy who's dating anymore. People are always trying to start a buzz about the rich and famous." Cassandra bit off her oyster and took a sip from her red wine as her words sank in, painfully.

"Well, thanks for increasing my anxiety level about it, Cassandra. Thank you very much." I twirled my straw around in my iced tea.

"I'm right, though," she said.

"You are. But how do I tell her? Will she understand if I say the reason I'm not with my sick wife is that she asked me to divorce her?"

Cassandra sighed. "I think, as long as you're honest, any reasonable woman will understand what you've gone through, Rusty. If not, then that's her loss."

"She's reasonable," I said and then recalled the way she dumped her last boyfriend over his lies. I wasn't exactly lying, but the omission was just as unfortunate, I supposed. "I just don't want to lose her. That much, I know."

Cassandra rested her small hand atop of mine. "Just tell her, boss. The chips will fall where they may."

"I can't trust letting the chips fall. Not this time. I can't lose another woman I love."

"Whoa, Earth to Rusty. Is this my boss speaking?" she asked. "The head boss in charge of the tech world? The man that millions of men wish they could be? The go-to guy? Wow, this lady must be made of solid gold. So, where did you meet her?"

I ruminated on Cassandra's questions. Of course, Kayla was made of gold; I had no doubt about that. "Do you remember that day when you sent me to go look for a dog?"

"Yes, I do." She nodded, prodding for more information.

"While I was out on Michigan Ave, I ran into her and struck up a conversation. In the end, I offered to take her to get a cup of coffee."

"Oh, the coffee date you had me set up! I remember that now."

"We've seen each other a lot since then. I can't get enough of her—physically, mentally, or emotionally. I always want to be around her. Hell, it's getting to the point where I will shorten my workdays just to see her and you know that's not like me. I'll work from sun up to sundown usually, but there's something about her that's magnetic."

"Rusty," she said and paused with the saddest look in her eyes.

"What is on your mind?"

"You have to tell her about Paula. You can't let this go on any further. It sounds like she's too important to find out any other way. Trust me."

"I know I have to tell her. It's just..." I didn't want to peel back the sore and hurt again.

"The topic is touchy, close to your heart? It hurts discussing what happened with Paula, I know. But think of it like this, if there is any inkling that this girl is the one for you, the way she reacts will let you know. But if you let things go too far without telling her, then it's all on you, boss."

"Then, it's settled. I'm about to go back to my house and tell her now. Thanks for coming in on a Saturday to help me get this month's schedule together. I had so much I had to rearrange being that Paula could take her last breath any moment now." Pain— and I do mean gut-wrenching pain— hit me. It ached to admit aloud that she would soon die.

"You have qualified staff. We will handle everything as long as you need us to. Besides, I'll have you on speed dial in case anything goes wrong. You can believe that." She looked down at her phone and held up a finger. "Hold on a moment." She glanced at her phone for a beat. When our eyes connected again, she had a hopeful gaze.

"What is it?" I asked.

"It's Lorna. She said Paula's status has been upgraded from standby to stabilized. She will call if anything develops."

If I'd gotten the news that Paula was stable any other time, extreme happiness would cloak me. This time, though, sadness crept in. I didn't think about what I would lose. I thought about my beloved Paula, who had more days of misery ahead. Her chance to walk amongst the Angels delayed. "Thanks, Cassandra, for being by my side during this difficult time."

"I wouldn't have it any other way, boss."

We finished our lunch and went our separate ways.

Before going home, I went to the hospital to peek in on Paula.

"The pulmonary doctor was able to give her a thoracentesis this morning, so her breathing is much improved," Lorna said, coming up to stand beside me in the hallway.

"Oh, hi, Lorna. That's good news. I'm glad they were able to get the fluid off. Is it okay for me to go in and see her now?" I asked, somehow feeling the need to get approval as if I were a stranger in my forever wife's life now.

"Sure, as much as she insists she doesn't, I'm sure she would appreciate a visitor," Lorna confirmed.

I strode into Paula's room.

She was awake. Tears slipped from her eyes when she saw me, and she turned her head away from me. She wanted me to leave.

But I couldn't stay away as promised. I walked closer to her bed.

She weakly waved me away, her machines going crazy with different buzzing sounds. Her vital signs increased, and she started coughing.

"Lorna," I said as I ran into the hallway.

Lorna grabbed her stethoscope off the counter. "On my way."

Doctors and nurses alike rushed toward Paula's room.

Standing outside her window, one hand against the pane, I watched until they stabilized her once again. I left before Lorna could come outside and update me on her status. I knew I caused her to get upset and that I had to honor her wishes and let her live out her last days without the pain of seeing my face. It hurt me to know that I brought her so much agony. Just the sight of me nearly killed her.

On the inside, a loud roar of cries rumbled in my spirit, desperate for an escape. I dared not let one single tear fall. I already cried more than a man should cry. Or had I? How many tears were too many when you'd lost someone you loved? Losing Paula was the hardest thing I'd ever had to endure.

This had been the hurt she didn't want for me...I had to move on. I texted Kayla telling her, I was ready to meet her parents.

CHAPTER TWENTY-TWO

KAYLA

The Deal

"Can I drive your Porsche to the airport? I've never driven one of these cars. I want to get behind the wheel and just see how it feels to operate one," I said to Rusty. We were in the bathroom, getting dressed for our trip to Alabama after he told me he realized how important this visit was to me and canceled his business trip.

"If that's all you want, then of course. Be careful with it, though. It's small, but it has a lot of power under the hood."

I smiled at him. "I can handle a lot of power."

"Indeed, you can. Now, come on. Let's go."

We took the elevator down to the parking garage. Underneath a sign that read "RVS" were three of Rusty's cars: a turquoise Porsche, a navy blue Maserati, and a gray BMW SUV.

He tossed me the keys to the Porsche and opened the driver's door. "Okay, I have one rule."

"What's that?" I asked as I caught the keys.

"Be careful."

"That one is easy," I said as I slid into the plush seats of the luxury car. I looked at the dash at all of the dials and almost got overwhelmed. *It's just a car.*

"Alright, fire her up," he said, once he was on the passenger's side.

I cranked the car and put it in reverse. We were off to the airport, which was about five minutes away from his penthouse.

"You're handling it pretty well, so far," he said as I pulled onto the boulevard.

"It's not my first time driving, okay?"

"Yeah, but this car has 200 mph on the dash. Even I'm cautious in it, and I drive it quite a bit." He looked uneasy.

I winked at him. "I have it under control, Mister." I ignored my buzzing cell and continued driving until a few minutes later when it sounded again. "Who's calling me?" I asked rhetorically as I picked up the phone.

The light turned green, so I took off, using one hand to steer and the other to unlock my phone. As I got the phone unlocked, a car that was supposed to stop at the red light crossed into the intersection. I looked up from my phone and stopped abruptly, missing the offending vehicle by a hair.

"What the hell are you doing?" Rusty hollered. "You could have caused an accident!"

The rush of the near accident sent blood pulsing through my veins. I was at a loss of words when I replied, "I—they came across when my light was green."

"No! The problem was that you were on your phone, not paying a-fucking-tention! You could have gotten hurt trying to answer that blasted phone. What in the hell are you thinking, Kayla? Do you not know how precious human life is and that you could lose it at any second? End up in a hospital fighting a losing battle for your health. You could end up on a ventilator for years! You could have to have fluid suctioned from your lungs just so you can have room for air to breathe!"

The wild look in his eyes scared me. "Listen, I was wrong, but please stop yelling at me."

"No, I will not stop yelling. Not until you tell me what you were thinking. Is anything that's on that phone more important than your life...your ability to walk...talk...be here for me?"

"But we didn't die. We didn't crash. They crossed over, and I missed them. It could have been worse, but it wasn't. Besides, that incident could have happened even if I didn't have the phone out. They were in the wrong."

"But it did happen with the phone out. That's the reason you weren't paying attention to the other cars. You can't be doing that, Kayla. That's careless of your life and others on the road. You have to pay attention. Driving is too dangerous for you to try to check your cell phone. Can't you see that?" he asked.

"Yes, and I'm sorry, okay?"

"No, don't be fucking sorry, be careful. I asked you to be careful before we left. Now, pull over right now and get over here on the passenger side. Let me drive us there safely since I'm the only one who seems to think safety is important."

I drove over to the shoulder of the road and got out, slamming the door behind me. I felt like shit and just wanted to tell him to take me home and forget the whole trip. Storming around to the passenger door, I flung it open. "Take me home," I demanded.

Rusty caught my arm. After a few seconds, he let out a deep sigh. "Kayla, look. I'm sorry for talking to you that way. I still want to meet your parents."

"No, don't take it back now. You said what you meant. I'm sorry for checking my phone, but I don't appreciate the tone you took with me." My lips trembled as I spoke. Tears welled up in my eyes.

"Come here, baby. I lost someone very close to me because of an accident. I just don't want anything to happen to you. Can't you see that? What I said might have come out nasty, but that wasn't my intent."

"Rusty, I understand that I made a mistake. I messed up, but you hollered at me like you hated me or something. I've been trying to figure out your mood swings for a long time now, and I can't."

"I just don't want anything to ever happen to you. I don't know if I could make it if I lost you." He pulled me into his arms and held me. "I love you," he said, pulling back to look into my eyes. "Don't you know that?"

"I love you too," I said, as much as I hated to admit it.

"Now, will you accept my apology for yelling? I'd like very much for you to drive us to the airport so that we can leave to meet your parents now."

I sighed. His apology sounded genuine. "Only if you accept my apology for driving reckless. I should've waited to check my messages," I conceded again.

"Apology accepted, but baby, please, be careful."

"I will. I'll always be here for you, Rusty. Always," I assured him.

*

"Thanks for agreeing to meet my parents. We've only known each other a little over a month, so you don't have to do this if you don't want to," I said as we pulled up to my parents' home. I wanted to give him one last chance to back out if he had any reservations about taking this next step.

"I don't have much family, so I'm honored to meet yours," he assured. He hopped out of the car and walked around to open my door.

We hiked up the inclining driveway to my parents' shabby house. Rusty didn't appear to recognize the imperfections of the less than humble abode my parents had called home for years. It wasn't as flashy as his Upper East Side loft, but the house I grew up in had a lot of love inside.

"Don't look at me like that, Kayla. I don't think I'm better than you or your parents," he said, reading my mind like a book.

"I didn't exactly think you thought you're better than us. It's just that my parents are very frugal. Some would say they are minimalists."

"Yeah, well, where I come from, I would have loved it if the worst my family was called were minimalists," he replied. "You wouldn't believe I grew up in the worst slum ever and that my parents worked their lives away to give me that bare minimum."

"I wish they could have lived to see you today," I said, reaching up to touch the side of his face. He was so sincere. How could I not love this man?

"I've come to terms with the fact that they are in the best place possible. At least, I know they're resting peacefully without the cares of this harsh world," he said, smiling up to the heavens.

The front door screeched open just as I reached up to pull his lips down upon mine, and Mama spoke, "Kayla, hello, sweetheart! I guess it takes meeting a new fella for you to come and visit your poor mama." She stood there in an orange pantsuit, her shiny gray hair combed to the back and hanging along her neckline. Her hands were planted on her copious hips, and her piercing eyes scrutinized Rusty and me.

We slowly stepped away from one another and greeted her.

"Hello, Mama." I wrapped my arms around her neck and gave her a big hug.

"I thought I would never get another one of your hugs again. Why are you such a stranger?" Mama fussed.

"I talk to you once a week, sometimes three or four times a week, so we're always in touch, Mama," I said. I missed her, but don't get it twisted. Drama was her middle name. I was prepared for her to make a big deal of meeting Rusty, seeing us kissing and well...just about everything.

"I enjoy talking with you on the phone, daughter, but nothing beats seeing you face to face," she said, pulling me into another hug. "Now, who do we have here?" Mama asked as she pulled away and looked at Rusty.

"This is Rusty. Rusty, meet my mom."

Rusty stepped forward, took my mother's hand into his, and squeezed it before pulling her into a hug. "I'm honored to meet the woman who created Kayla. I thank you for crafting such a beautiful woman."

Mama giggled.

I'd never seen her blush all the days of my life, but there she stood gushing over Rusty's every word.

"You're a good one, young man. Come on in here." She smiled at me as we walked by her, giving me the thumbs up.

Dad entered the room from the hallway. "Lord, woman, the way you're up here giggling you'd think Richard Pryor done came back to life or something. What's so damn funny?"

"Hi, Dad," I cut off his rant. My father could go on ranting and raving if unchecked. I could only pray Rusty's first time meeting my parents didn't devolve into a shitshow.

"Well, if it ain't my only daughter. Get over here, girl!" He tugged me over to him to rub his knuckles against my hair. Once it was disheveled and surely, a hot mess, he let me go and squeezed me into a tight hug. "I missed you, gal. Afta while, I'mma take you out back and spray you down with the hose," he said before turning to Rusty. "Sum you need to know about baby girl here. She love to play with the water hose, at least she used to. Y'all come on in here."

Rusty reached out his hand to Dad, but he was already walking into the kitchen by that time.

I took Rusty's extended hand into mine and gave him a slight nod.

He looked utterly bewildered as his eyebrow rose, and he searched my eyes for answers to my father's behavior.

"Dad, Rusty was trying to shake your hand before you walked off," I said, nudging him to be polite with my stare.

"Oh, I know, but uh... we about to eat dinner. Let's hold off on all the germ swapping 'til we eat, okay? I'll grill you over dinner, son. Then, I'll know if you're a good man for my daughter and if I want to exchange hand germs witcha," he said with a straight face. Like what he'd just said was some kind of gentleman's etiquette he'd pulled out of his ass.

A thumping sound started in my temples. This would be an interesting dinner. I looked at Rusty with an apology in my eyes. He was my invited guest, and my father had been rude to him. Although he was an equal opportunity rude ass, I felt horrible. "Now, Dad, Rusty is a good man and he's my guest," I spoke up in his defense.

"Well, what y'all in a rush for? We gon' be here a while. Sit down and let's have dinner." He turned to my

194

mother. "Francis, this here table laid out with food. You did that, baby." Dad took a seat at the head of the table.

Mama followed suit.

I remember when she would've protested, but she didn't even say anything about dad's behavior anymore. She just went with the flow.

"Mr. Johnson, I love your daughter. I'd like for you to give me a fair chance," Rusty announced, standing in front of his chair.

Dad scoffed. "Did you ask me for a chance before you started romancing my daughter here? From the looks of things, y'all been doing more than kissing."

"Garfield," Mama said, finally stepping up to reel Dad back in. "Come on, let's eat before the food gets cold."

"Fair enough," Rusty said, pulling my chair out to take a seat at the worn-out kitchen table my parents had since I was a little girl.

The tabletop was decorated with glass dishes filled with baked chicken, macaroni, cornbread, green beans, and a fresh pitcher of lemonade. Our plating was atop the vintage star-braided placemats Mama absolutely adored.

"So you got any kids?" my father started with Rusty.

"No, sir, no children."

"Felonies?"

"No, sir, never been to jail a day of my life."

"Pay your tithes?"

Rusty dropped his fork onto his plate. "Yes, I do pay my tithes."

"Wife?"

"Uh..." Rusty looked at my parents and me.

"Daddy, stop it!"

"Let the man answer the question," he said.

I glanced at Rusty as we all waited for his reply.

"No, sir, I don't have a wife," he said, his voice thick as he gazed at me.

I didn't miss the woefulness that entered his eyes. Maybe it hadn't been the right time to meet my parents.

"Well, that's good." Dad's hard exterior cracked and he started laughing. "There was this guy back in Vietnam who everyone thought was in love with his girl back home, but turned out that he was having all kinds of children over in Nam. By the time we left out from over there, he had thirteen children."

"That's terrible," Rusty said, laughing awkwardly. "I wouldn't want that many children."

"Well, it ain't got to be that many. Even having one that Kayla doesn't know about is too many." Dad stared at Rusty with a serious face, and when he saw that Rusty was uncomfortable, he said, "I'm just messing with you, ole' Rusty. I didn't think I'd be saying this, but you might be all right. Make sure you take care of my daughter."

"We're just dating, Dad," I cut in. "I take care of myself."

"I can respond, Kayla," Rusty assured me before turning to Dad. "Mr. Johnson, when I met Kayla, I wasn't looking for anyone to love. But as I got to know her, I couldn't help but love her. As I sit here today, I can assure you that I care about Kayla. Hell, I love her. I will do my best to make sure that nothing happens to her, and when the time comes for me to take care of her as mine, I will."

Mom sighed and raised her right hand to her heart. "Aw, Garfield, isn't this just lovely? Our little girl done found a man to love her with the intensity of a soldier at war."

"I'm not sure I'd say all that." My dad stood from his seat and walked around to shake Rusty's hand. "You, son, deserve a handshake for that speech, though. With this handshake, know that it's more than just two random people greeting. Know that it's a deal being made. One where you declared how you feel 'bout my daughter and that you won't hurt her or lead her astray," Dad stated, unsmiling.

"Deal." Rusty shook my father's hand and smiled at me.

I melted. Just dissolved like molten putty.

"Time ah tell the entire story, though," Dad said. "Betta make it a good one."

"I will, sir. You will see," Rusty assured my father as he looked into my eyes.

CHAPTER TWENTY-THREE

RUSTY

Crossroads

"Meeting your parents was...interesting," I told Kayla as my jet ascended into the air to take us back to Chicago.

She slapped a hand against her forehead. "Aw, man, I should have forewarned you about them. But every single time I introduce them to someone, I think they're going to do better."

"They can only be who they are and I like them. They're authentic."

"Well, that's for sure." Kayla chuckled.

"I learned a lot from this trip," I told her.

"Like what?" she asked curiously.

"Now, I know what to do with you once summer rolls back around."

Her eyebrows furrowed as she tried to figure out what I was talking about. "What are you going to do in the summer?" she asked.

"Spray you down with the water hose." I chuckled loudly.

"Oh, I see you have all the jokes! Oh, my God," she said, hitting me on the shoulder. "My dad talks entirely too much."

We shared several hearty laughs as we talked more about our Alabama visit. When the plane touched down in Chicago, that's when I got *the* call that would change everything for good.

"Hello."

"Rusty, it's Lorna. Paula has gone down quickly today. The doctor is giving her just a few more hours to live if that. You will want to get here as soon as possible." Lorna's sniffles on the line made her news resonate with finality.

I pressed end on the call and sat stoically.

Kayla's smile faded as she became aware of my internal turmoil.

Paula, my heart lurched at the thought of her name. Unlike I thought I'd feel when this moment came, I didn't fall apart, break down or cry. I just sat back in my seat and my mind went blank. A still moment of peace rushed in and covered me. Nothing seemed to matter. Coming to terms with Paula not living any longer was tragic enough.

The Porsche sat just off the tarmac when we got off the plane. I moved on autopilot, helping Kayla into the car, getting behind the wheel, and driving her home at breakneck speed. I opened her car door and let her out. She stood in front of me, and I knew she didn't want to go in.

"Do you want me to come over tonight?" she asked, running her soft hand over the expanse of my chest.

I stepped away and closed the passenger door behind her. "Not tonight."

"Oh, that's fine. I'll see you tomorrow then," she said.

"I'll call you." I hugged her before hopping back in the car and speeding off. I didn't even watch her go into her apartment, which was something I definitely would have done had Paula's last breath not been imminent.

I broke every speeding law on the drive to the hospital. I hopped out and ran up to the fifth floor. Approaching Paula's room, I saw her lying helplessly on the bed, her eyes wide open. She was coughing, trying her best to hold on. If nothing else could be said about her, she was a fighter.

Shallow breaths seeped from her when I walked into her room. Her parents were too elderly to travel to Chicago to be with her, leaving the burden on her sister, who kneeled down at her bedside. Paula's feeble eyes sought me out, recognizing me immediately. This time, the monitor didn't go crazy. She was okay with me being by her side. That fact alone did my heart some good.

Lighting up like a Christmas tree, she smiled. Then her smile quickly turned into a sad grimace. She opened her mouth, wanting to say something, but only a cough escaped to fill the room with the certainty of her impending demise. "Russ," she said in a weak, raspy voice. Then, nothing. Her eyes spoke out the rest of her words.

"I love you too, Paula," I said, coming over to rub her thin hair, brushing it backward with my hand. "I will always love you. I will never forget what we shared."

"Live," she coughed out before she fell back onto the bed and closed her eyes.

Buzzers sounded off, and her shallow breaths withered down until they were no more. Seconds later, the heart monitor went from a weak squiggly line to a flat line.

I fell to my knees. The dreaded moment came and nothing felt real. Not Paula. Not the doctors. Not the sound of alarm bells. Not her sister crying inconsolably. Not even the tears falling on my blazer. My beloved Paula, my first wife, a forever love of my life, was gone.

*

"Live," were Paula's final words, but how did she expect me to live when a part of me had just died?

Kayla's vibrant smile flashed through my mind with the answer to my question. I walked to my car, sad about Paula leaving me behind. But I felt ready to walk into my destiny and move forward with Kayla.

For now, I needed some time alone. How I made it home was a mystery. I couldn't recall anything about the drive. My mind was numb as I walked through the parking deck, trekked the stairs, and entered my front door.

I headed straight to my office and pulled out the chest, where I kept Paula's letter, along with a few of her other personal items—her favorite hair clip, earrings, and her grandmother's wedding ring. I ran my fingers over her things. I felt the dire need to be close to her at that moment. The last meaningful communication she had with me was in this chest. I opened the letter and read it over again. One of the hundreds of times I'd read her last coherent thoughts meant only for me.

Knowing she'd poured her heart out into that letter hurt like hell. It revealed that Paula had given up on overcoming her health battles way before I did. She'd succumbed mentally to being a paraplegic with respiratory and stomach injuries.

I, on the other hand, had held on until the very moment that she took her last breath. I never once believed she wouldn't walk out of that hospital. I'd never even imagined it. As I re-read her letter in the wake of our divorce and her passing, I still didn't want to believe my wife was gone. But this letter remained a reminder of all that we were and all that we would ever be. Paula knew we were going in different directions, and she'd wanted me to move on without her.

To know the woman I cherished as bone of my bone, flesh of my flesh, would never stand on her own two feet, bear my children, go to dinner or make love to me again was sobering. She'd returned ashes to ashes, earth to earth, leaving me on earth to make sense of it all.

Live.

I grabbed my keys, hopped back in my car, and drove to see my jeweler, Raul. He showed me some pieces, and I selected a princess cut diamond ring with diamonds going all the way around the platinum band. Kayla was the next phase that Paula wrote about in her letter. That beautiful, spirited woman saw this very moment for me. Knowing her, she'd even prayed for it.

Live.

The finality of Paula's final word hit me. I leaned against the building and just stared out at all the cars passing by. Busy roads. People headed in different directions. Someone on those roads wouldn't make it home because of an accident. Someone would have their heart ripped to shreds because of that loss.

Raul came out of the shop and asked, "Are you okay, man?"

"I'll be all right," I said, walking away without looking back at him. I hopped in my car, took out my cell, and dialed Kayla.

"Hello," her sweet voice sang into my ear.

"I'll be busy the next two days taking care of something very important to me," I told her. "But after I finish, I want you to get ready to take a long vacation. I could use a change of scenery for a while."

"But Rusty, where will we go?" she asked.

"Leave that up to me. You just be ready."

"I'll have to call Helen and see if I can get approved—"

"Do whatever you have to do, but just know that I'm not taking no for an answer." I hung up and turned my phone off. I'd allow myself to sulk today, bury Paula tomorrow and the next day... I'd try to navigate life anew.

CHAPTER TWENTY-FOUR

KAYLA

That One Night in Russia

"Would you be offended if I offered to buy your parents a new house?" Rusty asked as we were sitting on an island in Belize. He'd suggested we take a trip for a change of scenery, and I loved the view, as well as the many surprises along the way.

I squealed with joy and hugged his neck. "My parents would be ecstatic if I handed them the keys to a new place. My dad might reject it at first, but even he would warm up to it."

"Then, it's done," he said. "When we get back to the states, get a realtor on it, and we'll get them into a new house. Either that or we can completely remodel the one they live in."

"Oh, Rusty!" I jumped into his arms and hugged him tightly. "That they would love," I said, holding onto his neck. Everything about this trip had been a fairytale, one I hoped would never end.

From Belize, we traveled to Switzerland, Netherlands, Italy, and even visited Russia for our final stop.

About two weeks into our impromptu vacation, I quit Naustram because Helen started leaving nasty messages on my phone, demanding I return to work. I wanted to go back just to calm the waters, but Rusty did not appreciate how she spoke to me.

"Tell her you're done," he'd told me, assuring me I wouldn't have to worry about finding work once we returned to Chicago. "You can use my contacts to get new business."

With his assurance, I took great pride in telling Helen I would never be coming back and neither was Rusty's business. It felt so liberating to throw the deuces up at her controlling antics. He promised to open a marketing division at his company with me as the head, so I was set.

The entire trip was magical, but our vacation time was coming to an end as we docked in Russia. We were out on the yacht Rusty purchased. It was a massive ship with rooms for both the staff and us. I never had to cook a meal or clean a plate. We made love with the fresh ocean breeze coming in through the window, blanketing our naked bodies.

The night before we were to travel back to America, we were in the dining hall enjoying a candlelit dinner when Rusty rose from the table without warning. I didn't pay much attention to him getting up. I assumed he needed to go to the bathroom or something simple. It wasn't until he got down on one knee did I realize what was about to happen.

My mouth fell open in shock. I wanted to say something, but my words were trapped in my throat. I could not formulate a sentence to save my life. Things were going well, but I wouldn't have imagined he would do something like this so soon.

"Kayla, from the moment I met you, my life has been filled with joy. You're the first thing I think about when I wake up and the last thing I think about before I fall asleep at night. You are the love of my heart. Nothing would make me happier than if you'd do me the honor of becoming my wife."

I didn't hesitate for one minute. I threw my arms around his neck and screamed, "Yes. Yes. Yes, I'll marry you!"

My every dream had come true. I'd found a man who was worthy of my love. He did what other men were not willing to...earn my love. We were happy together, and we would continue to be for the rest of our lives.

"Darling, you have made me the happiest man alive," he said and pulled me to him. "I'd say a celebration is in order. Wouldn't you agree?" He nudged my chin up with his thumb and peered into my eyes.

I had drawn in a sharp breath before my lips parted in anticipation. Warm ripples shot through me as his wine-infused breath caught mine. The taste was far better when drinking from his mouth. He drew me closer and moaned salaciously, the vibrations of his moan flowing down my throat. He cupped the back of my neck and deepened the kiss, drawing me closer to him as his fingers coiled into my curls, eager to explore my hair.

When he'd had his fill of my lips, our gazes met. He traveled through me like the warming effect of alcohol. I saw the need in his ocean blue eyes, drank in the sated breaths from his soft, parted lips.

"Kiss me again," I whispered, hoping to never forget how to recreate this moment... I wanted this and so much more all the days of my life.

CHAPTER TWENTY-FIVE

RUSTY

Liberate Me

I pulled her to me, uniting us by kissing the corners of her lips. Her hot, honey-scented breath brushed against my face as she said, "Kiss me again."

Pinning her back against the wall, I riddled her with rough kisses. Our tongues battled for position as we hungrily pillaged each other's mouths. I lifted one of her legs up, and her fragrant smell caused my dick to expand to its full length against my slacks. It fought to be freed. I quickly unzipped my pants, liberating it, and dipped down to enter her sweet center.

"I want this forever, Kayla. Can I have that, sweet woman?" I asked, holding back from drilling into her soft body the way I desired. Her tight pussy stretched to size, but it was snug enough to urge me to stroke faster.

She bit into my shoulder as her thick honey coated my dick, causing a slickness that enabled my fluid movements in and out. Loving words passed between us, heated breaths against each other's ear.

"Don't you dare hold back," I told her.

"Never," she whispered as she ground herself against me.

"Yes. Fuck me, just like that," I said as I thrust my tongue into her mouth to capture the sweet taste of her once more.

She continued to thrust back as I moved inside of her. I came alive at the thought of being able to partake of this wonderful woman for the rest of my life. Lord, I didn't know what I'd do if something happened to her and I lost her. This thought stirred something deep within me. Something that made me fuck her harder, pleasurable sensations shooting through me in a way like never before.

I could never lose Kayla. If so, I'd surely die a slow death. My hand slid between our bodies to touch her nub. On impact, her body rippled with vibrations, causing her to sigh into my mouth. She bucked back, a slow, hard rhythm that caused me to come like fireworks bursting in air.

I'd been liberated from my past and felt ready to start anew. That night, while lying with her in my arms, I knew there was only one thing left to do. As soon as we got back to America, I would tell her about Paula. Then, I would be free of everything binding me down.

CHAPTER TWENTY-SIX

KAYLA

Nothing's Ever Promised

The morning after Rusty's proposal, I shimmied from between the covers, leaving him in bed. We were on the yacht he rented for the time we would be staying in Russia, and I could get used to this place. It reeked of everything regal and old, old money. My favorite part about it was the high-post king bed that made me feel like I was sleeping on clouds. I never imagined being on a boat this big.

My ebony hips swayed as I walked to the dresser where the butler left the Sunday paper. "What are you looking at?" I asked Rusty, who was watching my every move.

"The most beautiful woman in the world," he responded without a second of hesitation.

A smile upturned my cheeks. I picked up the paper and headed back to bed to be next to him. "Why is it that, whenever I'm with you, I don't feel like a normal person anymore? I feel like a fairytale princess in a faraway land."

"That's because this right here." He pointed back and forth between us. "This is magic."

I fell into his arms and settled against his taut body. I opened the paper to the Happenings in Russia page, thinking I'd find something interesting to see before we left. There was a woman on the page wearing a dress similar to the one Rusty saw me admiring and later purchased for me when we first met. I couldn't help but think about the whirlwind that led to my current situation—my window shopping and his search for companionship.

I leisurely flipped through the pages of the Russian Herald, musing at how they had English translation in it too. I also realized this scene would be my life from now on. Just the two of us reading the Sunday paper and loving life thousands of ocean miles away from home. Maybe we'd have kids, adorable little curly-headed cherubs, a minivan, soccer, tee-ball...the whole shebang. I couldn't wait.

I wondered if the world would be cruel to our future mixed children, but still, I couldn't imagine the world without our unification solidified. I glanced at the massive rock on my finger, and just as I gushed out more excitement, I froze.

My eyes fell upon the Lifestyle section of the paper. There it announced the true meaning of love and sacrifice in marriage until the very end. A picture of Rusty von Strauss and some white woman I'd never seen before graced the page with the headline: *American Social Media Mogul Rusty von Strauss Loved His Wife Infinitely.*

My world stopped spinning on its axis as I looked over at Rusty.

He stared down at the article. "That's what I've needed to talk to you about. I didn't want to do it while we were on vacation, but I can explain, Kayla."

"Oh, you can? After you asked me to be your wife, you want to explain how another woman is already your wife?"

"She's not...not anymore."

"So, you've divorced her since this article went out?" I picked up the newspaper and read the date. "This is today's paper."

"But she's not alive and we divorced before she died."

"Don't tell me she's dead! Isn't this your face on this paper?" I asked, throwing it at him.

"It is me, but you're not listening to what I'm saying," he pled with me to hear him out.

All I could think about was the picture and words in the newspaper. "When the hell were you going to tell me you were married? And to pretend that she's dead, that's just ridiculous! I bet she thinks you're out here on some extended business trip," I said, suddenly feeling like the stupidest woman alive.

"I'm trying to explain to you what happened—"

"The only thing I want to listen to is the engine of an airplane carrying me back to America, and I mean right fucking now!" I jumped up and began throwing all of my clothing in a bag.

"We're not leaving here until you hear me out," he said, firmly. "It was the hardest thing I've had to face since I lost my parents, Kay—"

I stormed off the yacht and out into the thick morning air.

I looked around at the foreign land, scared and hurt. Refusing to go back in his direction, I walked away. I had my passport and my own money. I'd find my own damn way back home if I had to.

Damn, I never expected Rusty to turn out to be a worse asshole than Ju. At least with Ju, I knew to expect nothing.

"Kayla, come back," I heard him hollering in the distance behind me.

Finally, he caught up with me a mile down the road and said the only thing that would make me go with him willingly. "Come on, Kayla, get in. It's not safe for you to be walking aimlessly around Russia. I'll get you a flight back home in the next hour."

CHAPTER TWENTY-SEVEN

RUSTY

Weeping May Endure for a Night

I didn't want her to find out like that. I only took her to Russia because I wasn't ready to come back home and face the reality waiting for me. However, my worst nightmare came true when the Russian Herald caught wind that I was in their country and started digging into my personal life. As luck would have it, Russians were interested in the life of an American tech mogul visiting their country, and Kayla happened to pick up the offending newspaper on the day we were due to fly back.

I'd gone the entire month and a half that we were away without thinking about Paula. Her sister and I agreed to have a small ceremony that only a handful of her old friends and hospital staff were invited to. Her body was cremated and spread over the Chicago River, as she'd requested. Now that I was back at home, and without Kayla, that wound was opened again. It had been expected, but unexpected at the same time.

I entered my apartment and crumbled into a million pieces. I felt weak being back in Chicago, where Paula and I built our life together. God had reneged on his promise to let me have and hold the one person that was mine to keep.

"There will never be another you," I wept, thinking of my and Paula's favorite song. "You are loved and will be missed, sweetheart."

Now, I was alone with nothing but the grief I'd circled the globe to escape. The person that brought me sunshine after losing Paula was also stripped away from me. Now all I had was darkness. With Kayla cringing at the sight of me, I honestly felt low.

"God, I need you now," I said, falling to my knees. "God, why did you take her?" I said before I lost my battle with the tears welling up in my eyes.

One final time, I wept for Paula. I sat on that sofa and let it all pour out of me, as day turned into night and night into day...

CHAPTER TWENTY-EIGHT

KAYLA

Hi, Hi

"Tech mogul Rusty von Strauss mourns the loss of his ex-wife who had been battling paraplegia and other complications from a tragic car accident five years ago. She had been living in a rehabilitation facility before her demise," Pam read the details of the article aloud.

I was back in my apartment, talking about everything that transpired in Russia.

Pam continued, "And it goes into more detail of what happened to Paula von Strauss. It says she asked him as one of her last wishes that they live separately, and she had their lawyer draw up a divorce agreement, but that Rusty still visited her and made sure she received the best care—"

"Stop it. I don't want to hear anymore," I said. "He still didn't tell me he was married before, and that should have been high on his list of things to do before asking me to marry him. I told him all about my past relationships. I held nothing back."

"Maybe this was something too painful for him to discuss. The woman had been ill for five years. There's no telling how bad it hurt him. And look, the article says she wrote him a letter urging him to stay away from her while she was sick like that. She told him to go and find love." Pam looked sympathetic.

"That would explain his mood swings with me and the women's clothes in his closet. I always felt that he was afraid to let go of something, and now I know what it is. He was still in love with her," I surmised.

"Her clothes are still in his closet?" Pam asked.

"Yes, in a room that's adjourned to the master bedroom."

"Wow, the poor guy loved her, no doubt about that. He's probably broken over losing her, then losing you, back to back." Pam paused for a second. "It's sad all the way around."

I huffed. "I know, and I don't know what to do to fix it, or even if I want to fix it."

"You have been home a week, and he's tried every trick in the book to get in touch with you. Maybe you should go see him."

"I will go and see him, but I'm making him wait."

"Life is too short to play a waiting game. You miss him, so go see how he is doing," Pam urged.

"I do miss him a lot," I admitted.

"Go see the man."

"Fine, I'll go. But he still has a lot of explaining to do."

My best friend gave me a motherly look. "The same way you need an explanation, he probably needs you too. Go, Kayla. Go see him."

*

When I got to Rusty's house, I rang the doorbell, but no one answered. I knocked on the door, and it pushed open. I found him sitting on the sofa, staring ahead unseeing.

"There was nothing I could do to save her," he said when he saw me. "I'm sorry, Kayla, but there was nothing I could do. I just wanted her to be safe."

After reading the article in its entirety, I realized Rusty didn't give himself time to grieve after Paula's death. A few days after she was buried, we left the country for a trip that he didn't seem to want to let end. Now, it all seemed clear to me. He'd been avoiding what he would have to deal with when he got back home—his grief for a woman he loved.

"Rusty, you have to give yourself time to grieve your ex-wife," I said, even as the word *wife* cut through me like a knife. The ring he'd given me suddenly felt too tight on my finger. I wanted to be his first wife, but now that wasn't a possibility.

"I've grieved for years. Grieved because there I was, a man who had all the money in the world. I could buy any fucking thing, but I couldn't fix her lungs, and I couldn't give her feeling back in her legs. What kind of man can't take care of his wife? What kind of man am I? She died on me. She died. She fucking died. She died, Kayla. She died. She fucking died," he said repeatedly.

"If I knew what you were going through," I began. "I would have helped you through it. That's why I repeatedly

218

asked you to talk to me. I guess what hurts the most is that you didn't trust that information with me. You automatically assumed I would react negatively. I wouldn't have left you. I would have helped you through this"

Then, he looked at me instead of through me. "I'm sorry. I let you down too, Kayla. I just didn't want to lose you. I needed you—need you."

"I wouldn't have left because of it," I said, taking in his porous looking skin. He looked dehydrated and like he hadn't eaten since we arrived back in America. "But we'll talk about us later. Right now, I want to make sure that you're good," I said, going into the kitchen to get him a glass of water.

I came back and held the water up to his lips. "Here. Drink some of this."

He turned his head away from the glass. "I don't want any."

"Rusty, this is not a multiple-choice answer. Drink the water," I insisted.

"I said, I don't want it." He pushed the cup away.

"Drink it, or I'm going to call an ambulance and have you shipped off to a hospital for dehydration."

This got his attention. He drank the entire glass in a couple gulps.

I went to get a warm towel and washed his face. I brought him a sheet and told him to lay down.

He lay there looking straight ahead into nothingness for a long time.

Then, finally, he spoke, "Tell me how you were able to leave me for a whole week? How could you breathe without me because I need to know how to survive? How can you experience life day by day, hour by hour, second by second, moment by moment? How can you live? How do you carry on? I mean, since you walked into my life, you have swept me fucking away. Sure, many could say that what we have isn't real and that all I'm doing is fucking you, using you, experimenting with you, getting over Paula with you. But many have told lies before, and many have gotten it wrong. When I fucking tell you..." A burst of energy must have shot through him because he picked me up, thrust his hands into my back pockets, and rubbed the plumpness of my backside. "I need to be one with you again. I need to feel you. Not for the sex. No baby, I want to feel the emotions you send rippling through me. Feel this thing...going from you to me, me to you. This transfer of energy, all of it, is more real than life itself. So damn real, I never want to experience life without it."

My body betrayed my wishes to take things slow, to give him time to grieve. Writhing against his hardness, I moaned close to his lips, "I don't want to be without you either, Rusty."

"Kayla, you have to know that I want you. Love you. Cherish you. I made a mistake by not telling you the truth. I misread you. Got it wrong. But I'll do anything to make it right..." he said, and his mouth crushed onto mine, making me surrender to his plea to make things right. Hunger and desire passed between us as our tongues dueled for dominance of our sensual embrace.

"We should take it slow," I said as I kissed him with enough passion to extract his soul.

"Slow?" he murmured.

"Yeah."

He slid me back down to my feet and walked over to stand by the window. Looking out at the mystic night, the layers he'd built around his heart slowly began to unravel before my eyes. "I thought about Paula lying in that hospital as a paraplegic and not wanting me to be a part of her life. It stung. It was something I didn't want to reveal to anyone. I didn't want to talk about it. I didn't want to relive the pain, the suffering, the divorce, the whole traumatic accident. I tried to put it behind me and tried not to feel until I met Meagan. When Meagan came into my life, I opened up and tried to live up to the promise I made to Paula. I convinced myself that what I had with Meagan was love. I convinced myself that she wanted me for me. I did it all to honor my promise to Paula. Somewhere deep down in my soul, there was a discourse that let me know Meagan wasn't the one for me. She couldn't be the one. Her heart was nowhere near as golden as Paula's, so I went back into my shell. I didn't think Paula was right and that maybe I shouldn't be with anyone."

I sighed as I listened.

He turned to face me. "That was until the day I was strolling down Michigan Ave, searching for love in a pet, and I saw you. I went looking for a furry animal to fulfill me, but I found you standing there as if you were waiting for me to

221

come along—my true love. I enjoy the time we spend together. There is never a dull moment, and I crave more time with you. I want you. I love you. I appreciate you. I want us to make something out of this. The day we were leaving for Alabama and you were looking at your phone and that person almost hit us, I lost it because the thought of something happening to you ripped my heart out of my chest. Just the thought made me physically in pain. I can't lose you. Please don't leave me."

"I want to be with you, but I'm finding it tough to get past the fact that you started out not being honest with me. I'm relieved to know you guys weren't married, but you still love her, if you're not in love with her. That's something you would tell a girl before you ask her to marry you." I still wondered why he would allow his deception to jump off the pages of an article to hit me in the face when he could have just told me the truth.

We couldn't go back to innocent Kayla and Rusty after that. We would have to settle into a new norm. And could I trust him if we established a new normal? Would he be open with me in the future?

"Kayla, I will never keep a secret from you again. If you allow me to earn your trust again, I won't betray it."

I sighed again. "Your heart is in the right place, but I have to figure all of this out. One day, I'm in love and accepting your ring, the next day I'm reading an article about you and another woman. It hurts."

"Let me love you back to where we were. Give me a chance to show you what we can be now that everything is out in the open."

I walked over to stand beside him at the window. I held my arms open and let him hug me—a nonverbal acceptance of his apology.

He looked at me with sheer happiness. "Thank you for being the woman you are. I'll prove that I deserve your love. God sent you to be with me exactly for this moment in time. Let's start over." He stepped back. "Hi," he said with a smile.

"Hi," I answered.

"I don't deserve you," he said.

"Maybe you don't, but I'm here anyway." I smiled.

"This is what she wanted for me, you know? She wanted someone to love me as hard as she would. She knew I couldn't handle this on my own. She also knew God would send the right person to me, and you are that person. I intend to earn your trust, every drop of your love."

"You already earned me. Now, you just have to make sure nothing like this happens again. No more secrets."

"None. Never." Rusty hugged me close. He leaned his head back and said, "Oh man, I haven't had a good shower in a couple of days, so I think I should go handle that. But I wanted you to know I appreciate you being here."

"You're good. Go ahead and take your shower," I said as he turned to walk away. "And Rusty..."

He turned to face me. "Yes?"

"I'm here for you because I love you from the top of your curly head to the bottom of your silken ivory toes," I repeated something I'd told him after we made love weeks ago.

His eyes lit up with newfound hope and joy. "I love you from the top of your curly head to your soft ebony feet." Coming back over to me, he picked me up into his arms and hugged me tighter than ever before.

EPILOGUE

KAYLA

Earned

One Year Later

"Are you ready?" I asked as Rusty walked into the room.

Standing in the foyer dressed in a casual black dress and black slide in sandals, my hair was pulled up into a natural ponytail. I wore a natural look as far as makeup. We were on our way to the cemetery to visit Paula's memorial site. Rusty had spread her remains over the Chicago River, per her wishes. But he also had a place of remembrance for her beside the headstone he had purchased for himself.

Nothing made me happier than to be by his side. Paula was a part of him; she helped to make the man he became. Had there not been a Paula, I wouldn't know the Rusty that endured some of the toughest times and yet loved as hard as he could love. I wouldn't change one thing about our love, even Paula's spiritual presence in his life.

This time last year, I was distraught to find out that another woman occupied a part of his heart. As I stood by the door waiting on Rusty to join me, I knew that his heart was big enough to love me and cherish the memory of his first wife. I would always be by his side, and I couldn't wait for our wedding, two months away on Christmas Day.

"Yes, I'm ready," Rusty said as his eyes seemed to pierce straight through me.

This man knew me through and through. I wanted him to always know every part of me. "Let's go then," I said.

He took my hand and led me out the door.

"Are you sure you want to do this?" he said once he opened my car door.

I slid onto the smooth brown leather seat and said, "More than anything in the world."

He smiled at me and trotted around to the driver's side of the car. The ride to the cemetery was a quiet one. It seemed peaceful, almost eerily calm. As if nature spoke to us, it was even sunny out. The trees looked perfectly trimmed as we turned down the road to the cemetery. A ray of sunshine even gleamed down directly over Paula's larger than life picture of her, along with her favorite brush set, lipstick and shoes embedded in stone.

Rusty opened the door for me, and I stood by observing the beauty of her honorary gravesite. "Would you like some privacy?" I asked.

He took my hand. "No, I want you with me."

We walked over to Paula's massive, marveled memorial site and stood, both paying our respects. I found that he traveled to the river every so often and looked out at the water to be in the midst of the place she loved. He'd created this site so she could be remembered.

"Paula, you asked me to make my heart content. I'm sure you know better than I do that this woman sets my soul ablaze and has my heart on fire. I love you for having the presence of mind to know what I needed well before I accepted it. I can't wait to see you again on the other side," he said. "But I want you to know that my earthly angel is here with me, and she also 'loves me from my curly head to the bottom of my silken ivory toes," he said.

Rusty finally told me Paula had often told him she loved him "from his curly head to his ivory toes." While I didn't think much of it the first time I said it, he'd felt it was the confirmation he needed that I was the right woman for him.

I spoke up and said a few words to Paula, "We're both thankful for you, Paula. Rusty is a great man who loves as hard as he can love. I know you had something to do with that. I'll take care of his heart for you. I promise."

"Thank you," Rusty said, squeezing my hand.

When we were getting ready to leave, I recognized something. "Hey, there's a new plot here."

"I already had matching plots for Paula and me, so I purchased one more right beside mine. The cemetery will add the words to Paula's 'the first to ever hold my heart. On yours, it will say 'the last to hold my heart."

"You're so thoughtful," I said.

Rusty pointed to where a cloud shimmered in the sky. All of the other clouds were gray, but this one was glowing white. "She's smiling down on us," he said as he took my hand and led me to the car.

He drove to the gates, then stopped the car suddenly. Reaching over, he cupped my cheeks to kiss me passionately. At first, it was a close-mouthed kiss, an exchange of breathy air.

Then, I grasped the sides of his face, pulling him to me and capturing his tongue into the warmth of my mouth. He moaned softly. A guttural sound escaped me as his hands cupped my face in reply. I held on tight. We were heart to heart, with forever on our minds and no end to our love in sight.

THE END

Rusty and Kayla had quite the journey to happiness.

Do you think he was wrong for not telling her about his ex-wife?

Do you sympathize with Rusty's grief and how he handled it?

Do you think Kayla was wrong for how she dumped Ju?

Do you think Kayla should have pressed Rusty harder to find out what was wrong with him?

Please write your answers on Amazon in a review!